These Americans

A Novel

Aaron Paul Schaut

Cover Photo: Chris Harrison - flickr.com/photos/cdharrison/

Cover Design: Aaron Schaut

Special thanks to Carolyn VandenBerg, Paula Yagodzinski and Manny Torres for the help and inspiration.

Blue Max

301 Alten Ave NE. Grand Rapids, MI 49503

Print ISBN: 979-8-218-19907-4

For Michele, who would never leave her cats
and would definitely steal Roger.

"There was nothing to talk about anymore.
The only thing to do was go."
- Jack Kerouac

Prologue – The Nature of Gus and Lily (probably in the voice of Morgan Freeman)

Some of us, heck, by my account, maybe half of us, feel both internally and externally trapped in a very large void that has a little tiny door on the horizon. We always keep that door in sight, feeling that if we should ever reach it, we would be free. Free of what, you might ask? Free of the constant nagging our souls endure as we stumble, clumsily, through the survival of these modern times. Whatever instinct makes us uncomfortable in a world that, for all intents and purposes, is built for comfort is about as ironic a pain as some of our personal energies can sustain.

For less of us, maybe one-third of the former half, there is a certain guilt that is instilled in us at some point during our lives. It's a guilt that makes the task of reaching that door on the horizon seem less desirable or obtainable, as reaching it would create some sort of rift in the lives of everyone around us, including our own. Reaching that door would leave us with such a tremendous burden of guilt that it would steal away any freedom we'd gain upon reaching that subconscious destination.

Gus and Lily are both trying to reach a similar door at the end of the expanse. Both of them face unique challenges as they attempt to travel through the wilderness, but their actions and emotions are controlled by different instincts, probably rooted in some other trial they experienced on life's journey.

The following events take place at the tail end of one of these unique challenges as we inch closer, or perhaps further away, from the tiny, rectangular door.

Chapter 1 - Raise the Bar

Gus spent his formative years with Prozac and *Trainspotting*. He might have been considered 'just a modern guy' if the phrase was referring to somebody plucked out of the 70s. He was tall and lean, with a mess of brown hair that seemed to have a life of its own. His facial hair was always present, usually trimmed, salt and pepper, and with a bit more mustache than the rest. He was a denim guy, with a pack of cigarettes always tucked into his top left pocket. Gus had a thing for shoes ever since he saw *Down By Law* and realized Tom Waits' appreciation for slick footwear. Unfortunately, his love for shoes didn't extend to his piece of shit car. Originally seeming cool because it was old, had the appearance of having some muscle, and because it had an old AM/FM radio with big buttons that you had to push in with a click. In reality, it was a slow-moving, gas-sucking, billowing monster of a car with a barely working radio and carpet on the ceiling that had become detached. It was that felt-ish carpeting and, in this case, was held up in places with buttons and pins from bands he'd seen over the years. All those shitty band logos holding up shitty fabric in that shitty car. It did have an old metal slide-out ashtray with a lighter in it that Gus thought was pretty damn cool. It also seemed that when the radio worked, it only played cool songs. Songs that Gus liked. Songs that made him feel cool. On his way to work, Lou Reed was playing, and all the colored girls were going do-da-do while Gus mumbled and chuckled over the line. Somehow, even in these justly sensitive times, Lou's lyrics remained cool and okay. Perhaps it's the way Lou uttered the words. "Hey honey, take a walk on the wild side."

Gus had grown tired of being behind the bar, all that fucking neediness and loneliness that oozed from its patrons. He had been lonely before, but it had been a while. He had a girl for a stint now; comfortable, reliable, and good.

Counting tips and reflecting on the night's conversations used to be an embraceable experience, but now it was like an endless cycle of feeling sorry, a little dirty, and somewhat insecure. No matter what, it was just the same night, relived again and again and again. All the evening's conversations would be put to bed, and the next morning, they would have been erased. Those same conversations would all happen again the following night, the same exact fucking conversations, as if they were never had before.

Friday was the one night of the week when the bar attracted a fresh crop of customers who would fill the room with new life. Different faces, different vibes, and a little more juice in the air. Even better than Friday's energy was Friday's tips - the boost that made the job worthwhile for Gus. He'd often linger longer on these nights, counting his tips at the bar while enjoying a few smokes with a cold beer. Having a smoke and a beer at the bar, man, that was one of America's greatest pleasures. "Yeah, it's a filthy habit… fuck you," he barked at a non-smoking, Detroit Tigers stuffed bear that sat behind the bar. "What do you care?"

Gus locked up and jumped in the car looking forward to his night with Lily. He was in a good mood, feeling carefree and content. As he parked his car, he let a *Pixies* song, playing on the radio, finish out. He picked up his bag of Chang's Better than Average Chinese Food from the passenger seat and made his way up the steps to his apartment. Swinging the door open wide, he was greeted by emptiness. No one was there, man. Lily hadn't shown up at all. "Fuck."

Chapter 2 - A Single Drop of Rain

It isn't like there's not always some god-damn thing (mumbling out loud to himself) or some kind of pain-in-the-ass problem. We all like to think that we are good, doing good, being good. Most of the time, our reasoning is legitimate but can also be subjective and open to interpretation. Despite this, it seems that we are always the target of some coward. Somebody who doesn't have the balls to actually be civil, talk or make a practice of peace. There are unknown enemies hiding behind keyboards, politics, and civil complaints. One example of such an enemy might have been Gus's neighbor, Gene. Gene didn't leave the house much except to get some groceries or maybe tend to his lawn. He had a keen sense of everyone's comings and goings as well as a good eye for anything that might be considered a nuisance or disrupt his quality of life. The list might include letting your lawn get a little long, perhaps a lawn ornament that didn't suit his style, maybe an outdoor project that was taking a little too long to complete. The neighbors often felt a sense of urgency out of a fear that Gene would become offended and take his complaints to the city. The city would then roll up, inspect, and threaten you with fines. Meanwhile, you were just trying to accomplish your personal goals, be a productive member of society, and keep your hands busy with things that go beyond that of keeping your lawn a respectable three inches long. Yes, a bit subjective. The gray area falls on stopping yourself from burning Gene's fucking house down. That's the trick, isn't it? You are a good person until you want to burn their fucking house down. Same went for Lily. She was all the good and sunshine and rainbows until she ripped the scab off your face.

Gus was trying to find that fucking thing that would put Lily anywhere but here. Maybe Gene the neighbor knew? Maybe it was cigarettes? Maybe she had to get a pack of smokes and was on her way now?

"Maybe I need a smoke?"

It was raining and a little windy outside. This kind of weather might be a really cool backdrop for *The Crow* or *The Spirit*, but it wasn't cool for a stressed-out asshole trying to have a quality think with his smoke. It seemed that karma would always place a drop of rain directly onto either the tip of the cigarette or that one bit of exposed skin, which provokes a nervous twitch. This causes Gus to mumble 'fuck's sake' almost every time. Gus lit his cigarette as though the cameras were pointed at him like he always did. Flick of the Zippo, double cupped, dripping old school asshole. He'd spent so much time fucking around thinking about the rain and James Dean-style smoking that he had to force himself into, what he called, 'a patient cigarette think mode'.

Gus liked Lily. She was the exact opposite of all the cookie cutters in the cookie cutter 6 pack. You wouldn't find her in the gym taking selfies with the big headphones and little matching outfit. She didn't use acronyms or dope phrases. She had no aspiration to be a part of the arrogant and semi-successful scene. No collagen. She was not a part of any crap group that used freedom as an excuse to cancel freedom. She was punk rock without being punk rock. She mostly reacted out of an emotional response, a fight or die mechanism that was programmed into her synapses when she was born. She wouldn't classify herself with hip phrases or acronyms like PTSD or ADHD. She'd classify herself as 'fuck you it's none of your fucking business so get out of my face.'

She was probably getting a pack of smokes or ran into somebody she knew. Gus was always overthinking everything, part of his own PTSD and ADHD, assuming the worst.

He'd smoked 5 cigarettes, and every single one of them drew a single drop of rain.

Chapter 3 - Coffee

Morning brought a fresh pot of coffee and Gus was chain-smoking inside the apartment now. He poured himself a cup of coffee mid-brew, the magic hour of the brew, the heart of a pot of coffee. This was when it tasted strong and smooth and right. He glanced at his blank phone screen while tapping the heel of his foot on the tile floor, his knee was causing the mid-century, yellow formica table to vibrate. Several times between sleeps and panic attacks he had messaged or called Lily. Her phone was on, but there was no response. He managed to talk himself into the idea of dropping by her usual spots around town. That didn't come easy as he already struggled with the idea of being too clingy and had been forced to read about all the stalkers, gaslighters, and abusers all over everyone's social media feed.

To offset this mental pollution, he would first have a second cup of coffee and a few more cigarettes. Then he'd hit the road. The rain had succumbed to sunshine, and it was a decent 65 degrees.

Lily didn't really have a pattern and could be anywhere. She was a consultant. She consulted all over town. As Gus drove, sun glaring off of the windshield and his wayfarers, the radio was playing "Paradise City". Not really a hip song but undoubtedly catchy. He cranked off the radio as he pulled into the parking spot at her place, leading him to believe, right off the bat, that she wasn't there. He headed up to her place and let himself into the apartment.

Lily didn't consider herself bohemian, yet the many candles adorning the room and the scarves draped over everything would lead one to such a conclusion. Cats. The cats were hungry, and their water bowl was empty. If there was anything she wouldn't do, it's let her cats be hungry or thirsty. Everything else was as it should be.

"Fuck. Fuck."

After feeding the cats and giving Lily's apartment a final look around, Gus headed toward the coffee shop in her neighborhood. It was a place that used to be dark with shitty art on the walls and full of creatives: a bunch of heavy thinking, brooding, dark, emotional fucks who were chain-smoking while writing, reading, and talking, mostly about music, movies, or philosophy. Now, this place was clean and well-lit with shitty art on the walls and packed full of well-kept fucks multitasking on their phones, while talking about Pelotons or whatever. Somehow, the coffee in this, the latter ambiance doesn't taste as good. Smoking another cigarette, Gus started thinking about all the people, sitting around drinking coffee, enjoying themselves and looking so fit and so clean.

"How do all these people have time to be here and be healthy? I can't find time to consider consequences and health. Hell, I can barely pay bills. Did all these people stumble into some well of good fortune and happiness?

Do these people, all dressed up in expensive outerwear, somehow make a cut I was called last on?" Gus had a mind that wandered, occasionally into these either depressing or encouraging thoughts based on his current state. The state usually coincides with the tips from the night before.

Lily could have been here but wasn't. Both Gus and Lily knew the barista, so Gus asked if he'd seen her.

"No man, haven't seen her in days. Why? You stalking her?"

"Fuck's sake. Okay, cool."

Walking back to the car, Gus started questioning if he's missed something. Did she have plans she told him about and he'd forgotten? Did he say something stupid and forget?

Chapter 4 - Lily

The veins of America, running with grime and sludge while covered by sidewalks and shiny glass bullshit, bothered Lily to no end. She was both a dreamer and a realist. The really real always crept into her dreams and tainted them. She had everywhere to be and didn't want to be anywhere she needed to be. She, historically, could pack herself up and leave with very little persuasion. She never really failed at things but never felt like a winner either. It was here that the confidence resided in Lily that housed a "fuck it all" mentality. She knew she wasn't getting what she wanted right now; she also knew that not acknowledging this would keep her comfortable. It was a big life while at the same time no life at all. She knew a lot of people from all places in life. She could imitate their traits but was mostly unaware of the imitation. The imitation was accepted as real for those around her. She was surviving, going on instinct. There was no self-awareness here as self-awareness would be detrimental to her success. She was a natural-born influencer at the deepest level of consciousness.

Stacia was an acquaintance, a figment of Lily's imagination that manifested into living form. She pretty much admired Lily, like all the others, and flattered herself as a best friend. They had very little in common deep down, while on the surface, they were very similar, imitations of each other. Stacia talked a lot, all the time. It was mostly gossip about peers which, according to Gus, was a replacement for actual animal instinct. He said it filled a void left due to a decent economy, unlimited groceries, and houses with cold, cold AC and hot, hot heat. Gus was such an asshole.

Stacia lived on the west side near the Tip Top Lounge. Tip was low-lit, fitted with retro furniture, and had a small stage that served as one of the last vestiges of cool music venues in town. For all the people always talking about all the cool, old, and closed down music venues on social media, you'd think this place would be super fucking packed. It wasn't. Gus and Lily didn't go there a lot either, so they were really no better than everyone else. They talked about it, but it was hard to act on it when you were either broke or just tired. Came with age. Lily dropped in there more often than Gus, usually as a wingman for Stacia.

"I want to stop up to Tip, Stace. You want to go?"

She knew Stacia would say yes, and by asking, she was just forcing herself to go out. She wanted a drink but never wanted to be social. Forcing social interaction was a must as a consultant; she didn't want to consult anymore. Lily responded to her own request out loud, "I will regret this within the first five minutes into the night." Her friend Stacia, on the other hand, had a thing for this chick bartender and would never miss an opportunity to see them.

The routine was usually the same. They would meet

up at Stacia's place and walk down to the bar. It was only a few blocks away and walking usually led to some good conversation. There were also, sometimes, some good people watching along the way. This time, Lily decided to meet Stacia at the bar. It was raining and she didn't feel like being out in it. She waited in her car, listening to Springsteen on the radio and glancing at her phone for the text from Stacia.

"I'm just about there."

"kk"

Stacia closed her umbrella and the two stumbled through the threshold and into the bar. Stacia immediately latched onto her chick and Lily's five minutes became a one-minute reality. A dude sitting at the bar rail started giving her that fucking bullshit "I love you" look, a look you get from dudes who are usually very near to full-on alcohol poisoning and have decided, with absolute clarity, that you are "their fucking everything." This type of scenario could go a variety of different ways, but most times turns angry and violent. This violence wears many faces, but with these guys, it only rears its ugly head when enough alcohol has been consumed. It's the Hyde to their sad and lonely Jekyll that they portray during the day, while they are sober and at work.

This particular Hyde went the way of saying 'Hey, you!' as he fell all over himself and his chair, glass in hand. On the way down to the floor, his drink created a small pool of vodka underneath the chair's feet.

Stacia quickly ran over to her friend shouting, "Lily, what the hell is going on?" Lily shrugged.

"Time to go, man," said Stacia's chick calmly to Hyde who glanced up embarrassed and confused from the floor.

Chick walked him around to the exit while he stumbled and mumbled something about Lily and how he didn't do anything wrong. When Chick returned, Lily promptly asked for a Jameson.

Jameson seemed to be the universal booze for sharing a shot with the bartender. Stacia's chick poured three and walked the drinks over to the small table. They drank while Stacia gave Lily a shit look, presumably for cock-blocking, which was obviously unnecessary and completely out of line considering the jackass they just threw out of the place was the only real cock blocker there.

"What does it mean when having a needed drink forces you to need another drink?" Lily said, annoyed by the unwanted attention.

"What was his problem?" Stacia asked.

"He comes in here every once and a while. He's always alone and always gets weird and emotional as the night goes on. I've never seen that dude just chill," replied the bartender. "I'm kind of glad he got his BS out of the way early."

"No shit, what a fucking creep!" Stacia replied. "I'll be right back." She headed toward the bathroom while her chick retreated behind the bar to grab another round.

The second Jameson went down nice, causing Lily's anxiety to retract a little. The warm buzz soothed her throat while Stacia, seated next to her, was already looking far too happy. In the bathroom, she must have applied more perfume that didn't jive so well with her chemistry. Her hair also appeared taller as she was then really showing off for the chick that she was so fond of. Lily, feeling annoyed, offended and somewhat alone, was in a zone and knew she needed to be somewhere else. She thought about how it needed to happen immediately. She stared, through Stacia, at that little, tiny door on the horizon.

"I don't want to deal with Stacia, I don't want to deal with Gus. All this would do is keep me stuck. It'll take very little to stop me from leaving," Lily thought to herself. "Gus might say, 'let's do it,' but it would be followed up with 'we can start planning tomorrow,' at which point the whole thing would become motionless and closed. I don't want to allow myself to lose this motivation. It's only when this motivation rears its head that real change happens. If I follow through, I will be fine," she continued to think to herself while really feeling the warm buzz of the Jameson. The steady cymbal rhythm and taps and clangs of a drum kit on stage forced blood through Lily's veins while neurons lit up. Surf guitar played slow and steady, and each bend of the tremolo sent a narrative through Lily's nerves. She picked up her bag while finishing her drink, as though the music was the intended score for this very moment. She quickly and stealthily left Stacia at the bar with her chick. On her way out, like the night's script was following the score, there was some wild chaos happening across the street to which Lily chose to completely ignore, focused on her goal. She got into the car, started it up, and would drive through the night, arriving somewhere else by morning. She would be a good part of the way to a new chapter in her life's journal.

"I can settle up once I reach my destination," she thought. "Fucking hit it!" She peeled out of the parking lot and onto the street, opposite the direction of the cops.

It was raining out and from behind the wheel, Lily whispered, "Diamonds on my windshield, tears from heaven, I'm rollin' down the interstate… do do, do dee."

Kansas City would be the first stop. No more, no less.

"Lord knows I don't want to end up there. Where should I go?" Lily was still whispering. "Where do I want to be next? Nola, Austin, Albuquerque, fucking Mexico?" All of these places appealed to her. "I'll pick one tomorrow. Tomorrow I'll be new. It's been 5 years since I was a new me."

Chapter 5 - Barfly

Our pal from the bar, Jake, was his name (not Hyde), after leaving 'on his own accord', managed to find himself in the brightly lit liquor store across the street. As he drunkenly eyed up and fell in love with all of the half-naked girls in all of the beer advertisements that were crudely taped to the wall, he thought to himself about how he deserved more out of that night. He was also considering how the disappointment and fear, that led to more emptiness and loneliness, had been working overtime in his soul. He looked at a smudged and distorted reflection of himself in the angled security mirrors that crowned the entire store. The reflection put Jake in a real, one-of-a-kind, "fuck it" mode. Mind you, this was not like Gussy's "fuck it" mode, this was a whole different level of "fuck it." It was because of this very spontaneous "fuck it" mindset that Jake, on a whim, made his hand, his jerk-off hand, into the shape of a gun inside his flannel pocket. Yeah, he was going to hold up the liquor store.

"I'm the fucking devil, lady. Hand over all the cash, one pack of Camel Menthols, and this beautiful bottle of tequila." It was a fine-looking bottle of tequila.

Larry and Paul were both standing on the sidewalk outside, kitty-corner the store, just hanging out.

Chapter 6 - Larry and Paul

Larry and Paul got up in the morning, threw on the clothes they had worn the day before, and heeled their way to the old gas station for their daily 2-liter of Mountain Dew and to catch up on the neighborhood news. The gas station was a relic - a shed of a building with an angled front face. The bathroom was located not inside, but on the outside end of the building and required a key that would dangle off of an old wooden handled plunger. Inside, the little store was dirty, with paint peeling off the walls, and shelves stocked with more candy bars, honey buns, and Little Debbie cakes than any fire code should allow.

The attendant, a young guy wearing a Ramones t-shirt under a blue smock, earrings, and nail polish, was always excited to hear the neighborhood gossip from those two corn dogs.

"How are you guys doing this morning?" smiled our young attendant while scratching off an inevitably losing lottery ticket.

"Grrrrrreat!" Larry said with his usual enthusiasm. Larry happened to be a big fan of the old wrestler Hacksaw Jim Duggan. This relationship with Hacksaw was what always prompted Larry to hold an invisible 2x4 over his shoulder while crossing his eyes and sticking out his tongue as he greeted you. Larry, like Hacksaw, was a tree of a man with a very long and unkept beard. He could appear intimidating at first, but within three seconds of talking to him, it became quite obvious he wouldn't hurt a fly.

Both Larry and Paul were originally from the rural "up north" and had been placed down here, in the city, by their mother. They probably shared a room in an AFC home here in the neighborhood, but nobody really knew if it was an actual AFC home or not.

"Last night, the liquor store got robbed," muttered Paul. Paul was quiet, skinny, and probably had the same rat tail for 30 years. He had a pencil-thin gray mustache and a mousy little voice that you had to strain to hear when he spoke. Paul was the exact opposite of Larry in almost every way. It would be nearly impossible for one to assume they were brothers.

"Yeah, the liquor store got robbed for real! Hehehe!" bellowed Larry with an even bigger smile.

"Better them than me!" said our gas station attendant.

"Heck yeah," said Paul.

"Heck yeah!" shouted Larry. He had a tendency to start an exclamation on the upswing and bring it down from there.

Chapter 7 - Nine to Five

Stacia was a nine-to-fiver, medium height, and blonde. She worked for a smallish local property developer named Brad, who had a mad desire to turn the old vacant industrial warehouses of the city into beautiful and modern apartment facilities to which he could charge a premium rent. In order to do that, he relied on a lot of big-name investors who needed to not only be constantly stroked but constantly updated on progress and return. Stacia served as his marketing director, creative director, copywriter, graphic designer, account manager, and personal assistant. She generally put in about sixty hours a week and was paid a fairly moderate wage considering.

For Stacia, what was more disheartening than the pay was that no matter how many events she attended and how much ass-kissing she supported, she was never truly brought into the fold with the boys. No matter how much of her job's functions actually saved Brad's ass on the regular while also giving him the appearance of having some sense of class and appreciation for quality, she was simply dismissed and even made fun of as an 'overly creative and somewhat bossy bitch'.

One time, she walked in on Brad's boys club while they were talking trash and poking fun at her strong and 'bitchy' work ethic and 'bullshit' desire to succeed.

What they left out was that her strong beliefs and desires would all serve to keep Brad, along with most of his boy's club, in fucking check. She had to be his mother, as did, probably, his wife, as he never actually matured past the age of 16. The 'boys club' was more or less a group of business school grads whose parents had enough money to promote a dangerous and sideways sort of growth. Beyond all that, it just so happened that what they were building was good for the city as it created jobs and filled an arguable need for housing. The thing is, it's all done with a passion that can only come into fruition because of all the 'mothers' that each one of them had by their side.

Stacia, in turn, worked her ass off with the belief that this would all, someday, pay off. That she would be accepted into the fold and grow to be bigger than all of them put together. The only things that she seemed to lack was the innate ability to act like a 16-year-old jackass, a trust fund, and a very literal set of balls.

At the Tip, the bar was slow, which was average for a night like this night. The attendance mostly consisted of bands along with the band member's better halves. It took a little while, but Stacia and the bartender ended up lit, smiling slowly as they decided together, with the help of booze and the promise of weed, to go back to Stacia's place and make out. As the bar was closing and as the band finished loading out their gear, the two were finishing up a loose dance to Karma Chameleon that was playing on an old jukebox. Together, they loosely cleaned up the bar, locked up, and headed out. Chick asked where Stacia's friend had gone. Stacia, while excited about her conquest, stopped walking, said, "What the fuck," with a most concerned look. She quickly retreated from any concern, grabbed Chick's hand, and started singing, "cama cama cama cama chameleon" while pulling Chick up the street. They danced past some police tape while paying no mind to the cop cars lining the street next to the party store.

Stacia was gonna rock their fucking world.

Chapter 8 - Kansas City, Here I Come

It was dawn at the outskirts of Kansas City and Lily had to force herself into the parking lot of the Comfort Inn off 435 after a very long and quiet drive. This place claimed to be a "World of Fun" but to Lily, it was just like anywhere else. She spotted a Waffle House across the street, which for Lily, was the first sign of being on the road. Those giant, yellow square letters are one of the absolute symbols of being somewhere else. She parked her Mustang and headed toward the entrance of the hotel. The smell of the Waffle House instantly made Lily aware of her hunger. She grabbed her room key from a Wednesday Addams-looking clerk and headed straight out of the hotel and toward the restaurant.

Entering Waffle House, she was seated by another Wednesday Addams-looking chick from whom she ordered a cup of coffee while beginning to process what in the actual fuck was going on. She decided to carefully glance at her phone. There were six new messages from Gus, two voicemails, also probably from Gus, and six missed calls, again from Gus. She didn't look at or listen to any of them yet; she wasn't ready to start explaining herself. She did open a text from Stacia and chuckled at the selfie of her and her chick, naked and properly rumpled in bed, with "I hit that" stamped over the photo in big, bold, cartoonish letters.

The waitress was a natural beauty, not trying to be

anything else. She had that meth model look from the 90s that so many girls resorted to drugs and bulimia to achieve. Lily found herself lusting after her, fueled by a mix of exhaustion and the excitement of adventure. Lily sipped her coffee and imagined herself making out with her. "Can I get you anything to eat?" asked Kate Moss. Lily was fucking starving but of course wanted to order something sensible because of potential judgement from her server. She thought, "Ugh, fuck that," and ordered the All-Star special and a Coke. "I'll get that right in," Kate Moss replied with a seductive voice. As Kate Moss walked away, Lily glanced at her phone but decided to turn it off. Any connection to home would only hold her back, and she didn't need that bullshit, at least not yet.

Looking around the restaurant, the morning's patrons were not what she expected. It wasn't truckers and grubby looking folks; it was average folks and families. There was, of course, this dude sitting with his wife and children who kept glancing over at her. It was the obvious 'I'll leave my family right now if you make eye contact with me' glance. "Fucking coward," Lily thought.

The coffee tasted so good to Lily as she took a sip. There was something unique about cheap diner coffee. It wasn't actually good-tasting coffee but was unique enough to bring about a sentiment. It reminded Lily of being on the road during different times in her life; it was one of the tastes she associated with the excitement and freedom that comes with traveling.

"Like a refill?" Kate Moss uttered.

"Absolutely"

Chapter 9 - Dog

Outside of Stacia's apartment was this dog, whose owner called Tank. Tank is a bullshit name for any animal, so Stacia and her friends always called the dog Roger. He was always tied up to a lead and was always upset at the world but, in turn, was always happy to see Stacia. "Hi Roger, you handsome boy! How are you doing today?" she said as she and Chick were leaving the apartment. Roger immediately got into downward dog stretch mode, yawned a little, and wagged his tail with a smile while waiting for a pet or two.

Roger's owner was an absolute piece of shit. He didn't give a fuck about Roger, and over the years there have been several times that Stacia and Lily had planned to steal the dog away from this asshole. They've even confronted him a few times as well as called the cops. This dude, Roger's owner, appeared always drunk and talked a lot of shit but never had the guts to follow up on any of his threats, though he never seemed to run short of them.

It calmed Stacia to think that one day this dude would fuck up in such a way that would allow her to adopt Roger, to which he could live out the rest of his dog days in a cozy apartment with all the food and water and bones a dog could ever dream of. Regarding the idea of dog ownership, she hated the thought of the responsibility but knew that it would fill a void and give her a purpose. The fear of this responsibility is why she didn't seek out a dog of her own. That being said, Roger would be the exception.

Roger's owner's name was Jesse. The guy always had a cigarette in his hand that was half smoked and unlit and he smelled like old beer and natural gas. This fuck was who you expected would still be asleep until it was time to get up to cash his disability check, so Stacia expected no company or threats. That morning, however, while they were loving on Roger Jesse's door opened and the same piece of shit who was trying to get with Lily at the bar slumped out onto the porch. Looking rough, with a bandage on his head, he gave them a look but had no interest in recognizing them. The two glanced away and back to Roger, gave him a final goodbye, and began walking down the street.

Chapter 10 - Coffee Shop Number Two

As early in the morning as it was, Gus thought of the various coffee shops Lily frequented, and the second coffee shop on the list was this dive coffee shop over on the west side, by Stacia's place. This was a place full of introspective artists, musicians, poets, and dreamers. The age gap of the patrons was awesome. There were either very aged and talkative little groups of guys or very young, up-and-coming scene kids. There was no middle age here except for Gus. He was at the early end of middle age but old enough to be out of place. No matter how cool he looked smoking a cigarette, he'd never fit in with either of these groups and cigarettes weren't cool anyway. The old folks clearly didn't smoke, or they'd be dead, and the kids chose vaping or weed. Cool or not, there was still an ashtray outside, but it was rarely used, and regardless, Gus still tossed his cigarette butts into the street with a flick. It's his thing. Fucking cool. Fucking disgusting.

Gus pulled on the coffee shop door, triggering the jingle jangle of an old brass bell that hung above it. He approached a way-too-fucking-happy barista who hit him with the "How is your morning going, my friend?" question. This was nice to hear, even though Gussy was in a fucking mood right then. "Man, I'm looking for Lily, you seen her?" Yeah, Gus never had to question if people knew Lily because everyone knew Lily. One part was her ability to bleed encouragement and light to whomever she came in contact with, the other was her innate ability to be memorable. She didn't even have to try. It was part of her genetic make-up.

"No man, she hasn't been in the last couple of days. Is everything okay?"

The thought of losing Lily would probably scare everyone she had ever come in contact with. Perhaps everyone's fears were a detriment to Lily.

"I don't know dude. We were supposed to hang out last night and she never showed. She's not answering her phone and I can't seem to dig her up."

"Shoot, man, that sucks. she's probably just doing her thing. Try not to be too stalker-ish."

"Yeah yeah, okay, cool. Give me a large americano and leave a little room, please."

"Sure thing!"

Gus took his coffee to a table outside on the sidewalk and set it down to light a smoke. While he smoked, he sat down and stood up and sat down again, like anyone who had something important to do but nowhere to start yet. He picked up his phone and tried to call Lily again, but her phone was going straight to voicemail. Somebody had turned off her phone or maybe it was trashed. He texted her, and the text went green, so yeah, her phone was definitely down.

Gus was ready to make the next move but had to take a piss. He often thought about how coffee has always been a big part of his life; it was his soothing, warm, black nectar of meditation. He believed that aging would slowly but surely taint the flavor and the joy of an Americano due to the sheer number of times it would make him have to take a leak.

Back at the table, Gus dove into his contact list and searched for Stacia's number. He didn't keep Stacia in his favorites because having her number in his favorites would be a red flag to Lily. He dug her up in his contacts and shot her a text: *"have you seen Lily?"*

"…"

"…"

"Gus, you need to settle the fuck down man."

"Chick says you need to relax too. They think you are being a little too protective."

"…"

"…"

"Gus, this is Chick, you need to calm the fuck down man."

Clearly, they were fucking with him. Regardless, he responded, *"I'm serious, Stacia. Her phone is off, and we were supposed to hang out last night."*

He watched the small *"read"* text appear directly under his message.

As she read, Stacia recalled Lily suddenly disappearing from the bar last night.

"Chick, he was supposed to hang with Lily! She was with us last night. She took off!"

"Don't tell him you were with her; she didn't want

to hang out with him, or she'd tell him and clearly, she doesn't want to talk to him. I'd stay out of it if I were you."

"Okay, okay."

"Sorry Gus. Not sure." Stacia replied.

"Stacia, are you sure? I'm getting kind of worried."

"Dude, she's a big girl, she can take care of herself."

At this point, Chick grabbed her arm and started wrestling with her.

"…"

Gus wanted to smash his phone. Not smashing his phone was taking the high ground for Gussy. "Fuck this," he said out loud while still outside the coffee shop. "FUCK THIS!" repeated a gal in her 50s, who looked about 85, shouting as loud as her raspy voice would allow. She was rolling a cart full of possessions up the sidewalk that included a large plastic cat and an old toaster. She then followed up with, "give me a cigarette."

Chapter 11 - Give Me a Cigarette

As Lily stepped out of the Waffle House, she was semi-startled with a brash voice asking for a cigarette. The woman was wheeling a cart full of all her earthly possessions. Lily silently obliged before hopping across the street toward the hotel. She'd been up a full 24 hours now and knew she needed to get some rest before continuing her escape. She hadn't brought any belongings but was too tired to worry about it right now. She'd figure something out after she gets several hours of sleep.

The room at the hotel was okay, considering the price. Thinking about money, she had about $200 in cash and about $4000 in the bank. She liked to keep a little cushion just in case she had one of these spontaneous episodes. "It would probably be just enough to get me somewhere," she started thinking about what this meant in terms of getting started. "If I spend one thousand getting to my destination, I'll have three thousand left to set myself up. Where would this go the furthest?"

"Mexico."

The ambient sound of the traffic, paired with the room-darkening, thick hotel curtains, provided the perfect ambiance for sleep. Lily fell hard into the bed and would dream of margaritas and palm trees and Coronas on la playa.

Chapter 12 - Buenas Tardes

It was just about time for the late afternoon scene to open up and come alive with bars, restaurants, skins, and sharks. Gussy was starting to lose some composure, and the picture of him lighting cigarettes was becoming less and less cool. He needed to focus, needed to play detective, and needed to get serious about Lily's disappearance. He called Stacia again and asked if she'd meet up. At the time, Stacia was still basking in the glow of her recent romance, but Chick had gone home to get ready for work. They worked the Tip at four, and although Stacia is mellow, she wanted to see them again. "Sure, Gus, let's meet up at Tip," of course, she wanted to meet up at Tip.

"It's not going to be all about your fling, right Stacia?"

"No, man, and even if it is, fuck you, Gus!"

"Yeah, okay. What time works for you?"

"Let's shoot for 4:30." 4pm would be literally showing up as the bar opened. She didn't want to appear that excited to see Chick.

"Cool," said Gus, "see you then."

He hung up the phone but felt defeated knowing he'd have a good hour until he got to talk to somebody close with Lily. He never, in his life, looked forward to seeing Stacia. Hell, normally he couldn't stand the sound of her voice, much less the sight of her.

He put his keys in the ignition and started up the car. The Pixies' "Wave of Mutilation" was playing on the radio as he took off. The song and his emotions caused him to drive really fast. He was spinning his tires around dusty corners all over the place and was barely stopping for red lights. He decided to just drive for a while. Pixies cranked. A whole lotta fucks still given.

While driving, Gus thought about work. He didn't have to go in tonight and wondered if he did, how he would fare with all the same conversations - all the rosy, red cheeks and dick talk. He probably wouldn't take it well. That being said, there was a rather good quality about the patrons at the bar; everyone there was a good listener, and everyone could be a true friend when you had a problem. Everyone was, for the most part, searching for their own love to lose. The odd part about that is how easily the sympathy turned to roastings and then a good time. This was a strange experience that the boys were really good at. One might say that if you brought emotions into the bar, they had the bottle and a cork for them. Tomorrow would see Gus at the bar at 3 pm, and man, he hoped he could play bartender and avoid becoming a patron.

Winter can be brutal, with four or five months of weather seemingly meant to destroy all hopes and dreams. Daylight is short, and sunshine is scarce. The cold does everything it can to divert the energy you have toward tensing your muscles and gritting your teeth. By the end of winter, if you had survived the cabin fever, you would almost feel defeated. Once that spring equinox hits, there seems to be a light at the end of the tunnel. It's that first warm day, 55 degrees or above, that makes you start to feel your body exude its pain and become invigorated with energy. It was pretty warm now, around 65 degrees and sunny. You could smell the small city's funk, and people were out walking dogs, begging for change, and talking to trees. Normally, these signs of spring made Gus feel pretty hopeful. He's not immune to the response of spring - dopamine-driven romantic that he is, he always feels like he experiences spring better than everyone else. He'd always take that first spring drive, get some spring coffee, eat a spring hot dog, and go out to the beach to watch the spring waves. Yes, Gus is truly better at these things than everyone else, as his ability to appreciate life is unmatched. This was, in part, why his desire to find Lily was so strong. The boy was in love with her, and the loss of her could potentially ruin a year for him. He thought about what recovery would look like and just as quickly tuned out the thoughts.

Half an hour to happy hour.

Chapter 13 - The Only Thing to Do Was Go

Waking up in the hotel is always a peculiar experience. The smell of the linens, the scent of the room, the soft whir of the window unit. You can always hear some faint muttering out in the hallway but can never make out the words. It is a very unique and satisfying experience.

Lily woke from her slumber around 4 pm, feeling a tinge of remorse and contemplating whether she truly belonged here. Wearing nothing but her panties, she sauntered out of the sheets, eagerly anticipating the scent of the coffee brewing in the tiny pot. Hotel coffee was gross, but somehow still satisfied the coffee addiction while tasting good when traveling.

Lily had blonde hair, was petite yet robust, and had a body that some would say was somehow magically alluring. People wouldn't categorize her as ideal, in reality, she may very well surpass this. Waking up in the hotel, nearly nude, with the coffee brewing, made her feel sexy.

Pulling her hand around the inside of her waistband gave her goosebumps. She'd lay back down on the bed, air conditioning fan gently blowing over her skin, breasts, and lips. She slid her hand into her panties ever so gently and gasped for air. Her senses were on fire, and she came long and slow after only a few, soft strokes around her clit. She laid there a minute feeling the air and the warm sensation that had been evoked by her orgasm. The coffee would taste even better.

While getting dressed, she unplugged her phone from the nightstand outlet. She looked at it, and it gave her that sense of regret again, a questioning of her actions. She hated that feeling. It's like she had to make excuses to that little stupid electronic device that was constantly nagging at her. Even with it off, she could still feel and hear the notifications, vibrations, and dings. To her, this was a kind of technological PTSD she'd acquired. Fucking sucks.

She turned the phone on and quickly set it to airplane mode. She hadn't even finished her first cup of coffee yet and did not want to hear a single ding or vibration. Only accomplishing putting her jeans on, she snapped a photo of herself in the mirror behind the dresser. She was a little flush, her hair long and unkempt, breasts supple and lush. Looking at the pic, it reminded her of some '70s-looking photo. The kind of photo you might see in a hippie album sleeve. She approved of the vibe and pocketed her phone. The photo would serve as the headshot of new Lily. Her coffee and the imprint she left in the bed would be her birthplace and baptism. Kansas City would now always be that moment to her.

The hallway leading to the elevator exudes the aroma of every strain of weed known to man, all converging in Lily's nasal cavity. She thought it funny how frowned upon it was to smoke a cigarette in a hotel room but somehow weed was a completely acceptable alternative. This also made her feel slighted, but she chuckled at the idea of all these high motherfuckers behind all these doors. Near the lobby, she grabbed another cup of coffee and slipped out the front door of the hotel for a cigarette. This was another small pleasure for her: the fresh air, first kiss of sun, a coffee, and a smoke. This scenario served as a benefit of being forced outside to smoke. This was a moment you'd got to enjoy every day that you get to do it.

She decided to skip the car and skip checking out of the hotel just yet. She walked over to the Waffle House for an afternoon breakfast. Entering the restaurant, she spotted the same meth model waitress still working. Lily hoped the glow of her morning masturbation was still emitting from her skin. She wanted to feel sexy in front of this waitress for some reason. While being seated, Kate Moss smiled at Lily who then received an inviting "hey babe."

"Damn, she is crushing!" Lily ordered a coke and another breakfast. While sipping her coffee, she noticed the waitress kept looking flirtatiously her way. In turn, Lily would complement the looks with her own subtle glance. This went on for a while until upon receiving the check, the waitress asked where Lily was headed.

"I don't know," Lily responds.

"I'm about ready to get out of here," Kate Moss mentions to Lily.

"Congratulations."

"Are you staying around here?"

"Well, yeah, I'm actually across the street."

"Cool, you want to grab a drink later? I don't normally

ask strangers out like this, but I feel a real connection here, a real vibe, babe."

"You do, huh, Kate Moss?" Lily thought to herself. Lily was fucking enamored so with a calm demeanor replied, "Yeah, I'm in no hurry and wouldn't mind having a little fun."

"Okay! There's a cool little bar not far from here. Want me to pick you up?"

"Sure, I'm at the Comfort Inn." There were multiple hotels across the street.

"Okay, I'll meet you out front in an hour."

"Can you make it an hour and a half?"

"It will be a long hour and a half."

Lily bit her lip and slithered out of the booth, just inches from Kate Moss's body.

"A long hour and a half it is then," Lily said and walked out of the restaurant.

Lily needed to get to a store and get a change of clothes. The date was encouraging enough to do that. She had no idea what the fuck she was doing or what just happened, but it did feel good and right. She stopped into the hotel, booked another night, and asked for directions to the nearest Target or Walmart.

Chapter 14 - Roger

Stacia asked that Gus meet at her place before walking to their rendezvous at Tip. She was uncomfortable with Jesse and that strange fucker hanging out there this morning. On time, Gus pulls up to the curb and holds out for the last minute of "Hairdresser on Fire" on the radio. Roger appeared excited to see Gus. He bent down to give Roger a pat on the head when he glanced up, suddenly making eye contact with the strange fucker on the porch. This guy, not breaking his stare, took a swig from a bottle of Jim Beam. Like a dog, he was claiming his fucking territory.

"Fucking cunt," Gus mumbled.

"What the fuck you say?" said the asshole, unflinching.

Gus gave him a final glance while walking to the steps leading up to Stacia's door. She opened the door before he could knock and was, according to Gus's sense of smell, wearing a little more perfume than normal. It was becoming obvious just how fond she was of this chick. She did look nice, to Gus's surprise. On their way through the alley, they both make it a point to avoid any more eye contact with the porch guy.

Across the street from the bar, Gus decided to stop into the liquor store for a pack of smokes. There were still remnants of the night before, plywood over the window, some glass scattered about, which immediately triggered Stacia's memory of the cops.

"Hey, what the fuck happened here last night?" Stacia asked the gal behind the counter..

"Robbery," she said. "Just another fucking night living the dream."

The clerk is a very tall, very blonde biker looking broad who has pastel fingernails for days and whose skin is sun damaged leather. She appears to have tattoos spanning time from the day she was born to last night.

"What the fuck?" Said Stacia.

"Yeah, so the guy was pretending he had a gun in his pocket. Like I don't know the difference between a gun and bullshit," she laughed. "That drunk mother fucker ended up with my .38 pointed at his face. Once he saw that, he started crying about his shitty life and his crap luck with girls. Then he had the nerve to ask me if I wanted to hook up! Can you believe that? I mean, I must have recoiled at the thought because he then thought he had a good opportunity to come over the counter. He ended up receiving the butt of my gun to his forehead. My ol' man came running from the back and drug him out by his neck. The mother fucker decides to throw a brick through the window and starts spazzing out on my old man. Lemme tell ya; he got a pretty good beating until he finally run off. Finally, the fucking cops show up. Better late than never, I guess. Needless to say, the ol' man and I got shit for sleep.

"Enough about me, what do you need, honey?"

"Pack of Marlboro reds," Gus responds.

Stacia asks the clerk, "Was this guy about yay tall, flannel and faded brown hair?"

"Yeah, real fucking looker ha-ha."

"He was slopping all over my friend at the bar last night and Chick had to toss him. He was fucking trashed."

She realized Gus was standing behind her. She could feel his blood pressure.

"What friend?" Gus asks in a slow demanding tone.

"I mean — my acquaintance!"

The woman decided to interject, "Lily?"

Gus, "what the fuck did you say?"

"The asshole trying to rob me kept saying 'fucking Lily, fuck her... stupid name' and shit like that."

"Stacia, we are going to go across the street, and you are going to tell me exactly what the fuck is going on." Gus was stern and kind of scary right now.

"Okay." muttered Stacia.

"Don't let the door hit you in the ass on the way out!" the clerk chuckled.

Gus grabbed Stacia's hand and hurried her out of the store and across the street. He threw open the door to the bar and sort of tossed her in. Chick lit up as they noticed Stacia enter the dimly lit bar but quickly turned concerned when they saw the look on Stacia's face followed by her dark looking escort.

"Two Jameson rocks," Gus said.

Stacia mousy mumbled, "please?" and then mouthed,

"it's okay," in Chick's direction.

Chick touched Stacia's hand before walking around the bar to pour the drinks.

"Give me just a second, please Gus."

He let go of her hand and muttered "make it quick."

She dashed over and whispered to Chick, "Hey, sorry!"

"What the fuck is going on?"

"Remember my friend, Lily, from last night?"

"Yeah, why?"

"That's her guy. She ghosted him. He's been looking for her all day."

"What'd he do to her?"

"Nothing, Gus is a good guy, he loves her, I guess. I'm actually starting to wonder where she is as well."

"Fuck," said Chick, "You hear what that piece of shit who was falling on her did last night after I tossed him?"

"Yeah, broad at the store told us just now. She also tipped Gus off to Lily being here last night."

"You think that asshole had something to do with Lily going missing?"

"Fuck."

"Yeah, I don't know, Fuck."

Chapter 15 - Lone Gunman

Jake was running, limping, tripping, and holding his hand to his side. He wasn't sober or smart enough to understand what just happened. He was beaten pretty badly by the store guy and was a little dizzy from the blood loss. His flannel coat was pretty well soaked with blood from the deep gash on his head. While dragging his feet, he caught his foot on a chunk of raised sidewalk and went straight to the ground. Looking up, peering through the tint of red blood between the creases in his eyes, he found a dog's face looking down at him. Tank started licking the Jake's face. "Tank, get the fuck back." Jesse, Stacia's neighbor, bent down and grabbed Jake under the shoulder. He helped bring him up onto the porch and into the house where he put him on the couch to sleep off some of whatever bullshit got him. Jesse knew Jake; they hung out on occasion, and it usually ended with Jake in some kind of scrap. Both of them could very well have been in this situation before. The bleeding had mostly stopped, but Jake was gonna need some staples. He had a piece of glass in his side too. It wasn't terribly bad but was bad enough to become a problem if untreated. Because of this, Jesse pulled the glass out and taped a large bandage from his kitchen's medical kit on the wound. After tending to the wound in Jake's side along with the gash on his head, Jesse's ability to care for another human being was maxed out for the night, so he took his spot in his shitty old lazy boy, lit a smoke, and fell asleep. Roger was still outside.

The next morning, as the sun peeked through the wooden blinds above the couch, Jake woke up with a terrible headache. He made the mistake of touching his head. "Shit," he mumbled in a low, raspy tone. Coffee was on; he could smell it. He found his way to the kitchen but was still dizzy and was using the wall as a crutch. He reached the coffee pot and filled the nearest coffee cup. There was a bottle of bourbon on the counter. He thought about pouring some in his coffee but instead opted to take the bottle with him. The wall helped him back into the living room and out onto the porch. He spotted Stacia and Chick petting on the dog. He squinted, trying to focus on them. He thought one looked familiar and knew the other 'fuck hole' from the bar. Chick gave him a shitty look and the two took off. Jake, swirling and dizzy, slid onto an old automobile bench seat that was conveniently recycled as patio furniture and took a swig of the Jim Beam. "Fuck me," he murmured as he shut his eyes and started to sleep.

Chapter 16 - Date Night

Lily walked into Target, and the distinct odor of Target disinfectant and food court, and headed over to the clothing department. She wasn't being too particular. A couple of tank tops, one of which was a *Led Zeppelin - Swan Song* tank, some t-shirts, a couple of pairs of jeans, and other essentials were quickly grabbed. She also picked up some toiletries, a pound of Starbucks coffee, and filters for the hotel rooms. She was wearing her Doc Martens but wanted something more comfortable, so she grabbed a pair of red, high-top Chucks. She quickly made her way through the checkout and headed back to her car. She popped the hatch of her red 1986 Mustang GT. She had owned this car for a while and kept it very clean. She might get rid of everything, but this car would stay with her always. She tossed her items into the back and settled into the driver's seat. She chuckled when she turned the key and "Heartbreaker" was playing on the radio.

Pulling out of the parking lot, she realized she was at a crossroads. She had a huge attraction to "Kate Moss" and could really use someone unfamiliar to talk to. She thought about how the night would go and how the morning would feel. She remembered how she felt this morning. "Nope." She immediately headed toward the interstate south. She would not set herself up to ruin her memory of Kansas City and what it represented. It was not worth a hot and equally awkward date. It was also fair to say that she had moved on entirely from Gus. She no longer thought of him as someone she cared for. He was now a thing she would be rebelling against. So became Stacia, so became everything before Kansas City.

She stopped at the Phillips 66 Mini Mart to get a couple of packs of cigarettes, a couple of cokes, a Monster Mocha, and some Tylenol. She noticed that they had those highway maps on a shelf near the motor oil. She grabbed one, settled up and headed out to the car to fill up her tank. She unfolded the map on the hatchback window and checked a route. She was about 3 hours from Tulsa and decided it would make the perfect place to get something to eat and stretch her legs a bit. She put the nozzle back in the pump and set off. Tulsa - 35 South.

Chapter 17 - Treats

"Do we tell him?" Stacia took her shot with Chick.

"I think we have to."

"Chick, stay here, let me sit with him alone for a minute.'

"Cool." They filled the three shot glasses.

Stacia went back over to the table Gus was at and moved her chair a little closer to his. She set his shot down and they drank together.

"What the fuck is going on, Stacia?" Gus was calm.

"Look, we came here last night. I didn't know she was supposed to meet up with you, I promise. When we got here, I became sort of preoccupied with Chick while the guy that held up the liquor store decided to have a thing for Lily. It really wasn't a big deal. He Tried to talk to her, tripped and fell flat on his face and spilled his drink everywhere. Chick showed him to the door. Lily didn't leave or go after him or anything. She was still nursing her drink at the table over there."

"This isn't getting me anywhere, Stacia."

"I know, Gus, Chick and I were drinking and dancing and flirting with each other. She must have slipped out of the bar at some point. I didn't notice her leaving. By the time Chick and I left we were pretty lit and weren't paying attention to much. I didn't even notice the liquor store scene as we walked right by it. I'm a shitty friend, Gus. I'm sorry."

"I get it, Stacia. You have been a good friend to Lily, and I know you've been lonely. I know it sucks to see me and Lily go off and do our thing while you stumble home, alone. I do get it. Lily is an adult and has always been capable of taking care of herself, but we still have to find out what the FUCK is going on."

Gus had reached a small moment of clarity here. At least he had a little more of the story. He was definitely confused as to why she ditched him and doesn't like that she's not responding. Regardless, having this little bit of info, no matter how defeating, definitely comforted him on some bullshit level.

"We have to talk to that guy, we have to find him," said Gus.

"I know where he is," Stacia said, "He's the guy from the porch. Roger's porch."

"What the fuck, are you fucking with me?"

"Not at all."

Gus sprang from the chair and tossed on his denim jacket. "We're going... Now!" He demanded. Chick appeared at their table. "What's going on?" she asked.

"We're going," said Gus, "now!"

"I'm coming with you." they said.

"Fuck you are," said Gus.

"Fuck you, dude, I'm coming with!" Chick was offended.

As they walked by the party store, Gus looked toward

the broken window and thought about Lily. The scene brought him a lot of discomfort. He felt a little sick to his stomach and hated the feeling. Real true ache. Real god damn emptiness. "Jesus Christ." he said quite loudly.

They arrived at Roger's house. Roger stood to greet them with a prancing excitement. "Oh Roger," Stacia said while Chick gave the dog a pet on the cheek. Our guy, Jake, was no longer sitting on the porch. This put Gus into a real head-spin, he became anxious, and his tunnel vision had him headed straight to the door. He opened the screen and slammed the side of his fist into the door frame, several times, so seemed as though the whole porch shook with each knock.

"Who the fuck is banging at my door like an asshole?"

"Come out here, man. Get the fuck out here."

The door opened a crack and a voice said, dark and calmly, "what the fuck do you want?"

"I want to talk to the mother fucking guy that robbed the liquor store, fucking now!"

"Who, Jake?" replied Jesse, "Get the fuck outta here and get those 'things' of yours away from my fucking dog."

Gus responded again with, "Where is the guy that was out here this morning. Get him the fuck out here."

"Last warning… Get the fuck off my porch."

Gus heard what he assumed was a round being pumped into a shotgun chamber. He was frantic but cool enough to know that he had to choose his words carefully.

"Look man, I don't know you from shit, but my girl is

missing and the guy who robbed the liquor store was the last one we know saw her. I'm pretty messed up about all of it and wanted to talk to him is all. I don't give a fuck about the liquor store or anything else."

"Look man," Jesse opened the door a little more and said, with a Clint Eastwood like tone, "I don't fucking care. Get the fuck out, now."

The door opened a little more, enough for Gus to see Jesse and the barrel of the shotgun he was holding. Jesse was a big guy, clean-shaven with skin like leather. He wore an old trucker hat that said "Cocky" with a rooster on it. His eyes were piercing blue and stared right into Gus's soul. Gus muttered to himself, "This was not a man to fuck with," without realizing he was speaking out loud.

"You better believe I'm not a man to fuck with, pal, now get the fuck out of here!"

Chick yelled, "fuck you, man!" from Roger and Stacia's position near the doghouse, "Just tell us where the fuck he is!"

Jesse kicked the door wide and pointed the gun at them. They quickly looked down at the ground. His hat should have belonged to Chick at that moment of confrontation. They were really fucking cocky and apparently have balls of steel.

Gus backed down the porch with his hands up in the "chill" position, slightly raised. "Let's get the fuck out of here," he said to Stacia and Chick.

They turned and walked kind of quickly in the direction of the bar. As they were walking, Larry and

Paul yelled, "Hi, Rae!" from across the street. Chick threw up a hand while continuing to speed walk.

"Fuck me," said Gus, "We need to find this guy."

Arriving at the bar, Chick spotted a motorcycle that had been there since the day before.

"What the fuck is going on, Chick?" yelled a regular who had been standing by the door waiting for the bar to become open.

"Hold the fuck up!" yelled Chick.

"Wait a fucking second." they said. "That bike was there yesterday. I wonder if it's that fucking guy's bike?"

Gus lightly grabbed Stacia's wrist and pulled her quickly toward the bike. He looked down at it for a second. The bike had a couple of leather saddlebags that were held closed by a couple of clips on either side. He opened the left one. "Nothing," he said. Chick opened the other one, gave a smirking glance toward Gus and said, "what the fuck do you know!" Sticking out of a tool roll was a piece of paper. It was a registration. "Jake Allen Tomachewski," Chick said, surprised that finding a name would be so easy. "The guy at the house said Jake when he answered the door. He fucking said Jake," said Gus. "We fucking got him."

They, including our patron, went into the bar. Chick ran around the back of the bar to pour drinks. Our patron friend sat at the corner of the bar near the door. This was his usual seat. Stacia and Gus stood at the far end of the bar next to the bar opening. Chick gave John, the patron, his Miller Lite and coke and headed down to the far end of the bar with whiskey for the three of them.

"How do we find this Jake motherfucker?" says Chick.

"Why are you so interested in this, Chick? What the fuck!" Gus was annoyed.

"Because all I do is work at this fucking bar, sleep and eat. This is a solid mystery. I wanna help you guys," they said.

"Did you say Jake?" mumbled John from the other end of the bar.

Chapter 18 - Tulsa

Lily hadn't stopped the car since leaving Kansas City. She didn't need to; she didn't have to 'do' anything. Usually all about the ride, she wanted to get to her next destination quickly. It was warm and balmy tonight, after she passed through a little rain. The moon was bright and clear, and the air smelled amazing. She felt so alive. She was pretty excited to get out of the car after the last couple of hours. She was still tired from the 24-hour stretch and needed to find a rhythm.

She saw a sign indicating "Route 66" and figured that this was the perfect place to squat. There was a Waffle House right off the highway. She briefly thought about 'Kate Moss's and figured, 'why not', while merging onto the exit. She pulled into the Waffle House parking lot. She grabbed her phone out of the back and jotted in. It was late, and there weren't a lot of people in the restaurant. She grabbed a booth and a menu. This time the waitress was definitely not her type. This was more or less Rosie from the old Bounty paper towel commercials. "Good evening sweetie, can I start you off with something to drink?"

"I'll have a coffee and a coke, please."

"Punishing your bladder?" Rosie chuckled. Lily enjoyed Rosie's stereotype.

"I try," said Lily.

"I'll grab those while you look over the menu."

"Thanks"

Lily stared at her reflection in her turned off phone. She didn't want to turn it on. She decided not to.

"Here you go, honey! Are you ready to order?"

"Yeah, sure, I'll do a BLT and fries."

"Good choice, anything else?"

"Nuh, hey, is there a cool Route 66 hotel I could stay at for the night?"

"Desert Hills is just up the road a little way. You can't miss it." Her eyes twinkled as she smiled, front teeth noticeably yellowed.

"It feels good to eat knowing that I will be in bed soon, in a different town, in a route 66 hotel. It feels right. I wonder what I might have missed out on with Kate Moss and if she was hurt. Maybe she didn't show either. She was so pretty," thought Lily.

After eating, Lily paid her bill, went out to the mustang, and started it up. She took a left out of the waffle house and pulled into the gas station. She grabbed some chips and a couple of cokes and proceeded to the counter. The attendant was nice while ringing her up. She topped off the mustang and once again headed west. It wasn't far until she saw the bright neon cactus of the desert hills sign. "Cable, Phone, WIFI" ha-ha. She hopped out of the car and up to the lobby where she was greeted kindly by a small but strong looking woman. She asked for a room. There was one vacancy left. It was "my lucky day."

She pulled the car to the room, unpacked the hatch, took a second to smell the air and enjoyed the sound of the neon buzzing before wandering in. The room was full of retro charm. Old retro phone, old retro fridge, and a big glass amber ashtray. "Jackpot!" There wasn't a coffee maker so the coffee she brought with her was useless. Regardless, this was perfect. She put her things on the small table, flipped on the TV, popped open a coke and started to undress. "A shower will feel fantastic," she thought. She grabbed her coke and headed for the bathroom. She bought a can of coke for this very reason. Shower coke. The shower was amazing. The black and white tile patterned out the numbers "66" and formed a cactus. "Fuck yeah!"

The shower is so void of distraction. Just the hum of the flowing water and your thoughts. Even so, the idea that she was making a terrible mistake entered her mind. The 'what-ifs' that come with a dramatic shift. It's funny that a shift like this could be forced on you at any given time. When you create the shift, you control the shift.

Lily preferred to control the shift. She preferred the excitement of creating the shift vs the fear and insecurities that come with a forced shift. She thought about this knowing full well that the shift is forced either way. She thought about the fact that she'd unintentionally forced a shift into the lives of Gus, Stacia, and anyone else whose life she had been currently impacting. "Not my problem," she thought. "I'm a survivor, a warrior, a fucking Viking warrior."

She let the warm water run down the back of her neck. She closed her eyes and rested her forehead on the tile. The tile was cool against her skin and the contrast felt wonderful. She tossed a towel on the floor and stepped out of the tub. The room was full of steam. Lily drew a heart on the mirror with her finger and wrapped a towel around her head and another around her body. She grabbed her coke and walked toward the small desk. She took her map off of the table, sat on the bed and unfolded it. She loved looking at all the names of places on an old school map. Seeing them in print made them magical and appear less reachable, further away. There were no distractions between the names, roads, and rivers. No walk score, no time to arrive, no reviews or ads. All the names and squiggles were left to what you knew, word of mouth, and your imagination. She focused on Tulsa and the cross streets of the Desert Hills Motel. With her finger, she tried to identify and follow Route 66 from Tulsa west. She wondered if she should change her plans and just ride the mother road. "Santa Monica, ha-ha. Yeah, no." She looked at Texas and Mexico and studied the shapes. Her eyes fell heavy. She crawled into the sheets and fell very quickly to sleep.

John, our patron at the end of the bar, had known Jake for a very long time. They used to ride together. John is in a club and Jake always wanted to join.

"I never liked Jake much. He was too fucking eager."

"You know who we're talking about?" asked Chick.

"Yeah, he always wanted in the club. He'd show up to all our events, at our bars, our rides. Dude was always a little drunk and always expected us to just let him in. Dude was looking for purpose but had no business being on two, much less with a group. He didn't seem real to me. Just a kind of beat dog. We don't have room for that shit. We also aren't babysitters."

Gus interrupted, "you know where we can find him? We're missing our friend, my girlfriend, and he was the last person anybody seen her with."

"I don't. I saw his bike out back though. If he ain't come and grabbed it, he's either in jail, sleeping it off, or dead. If he ain't the latter, he'll be back for it."

Chick filled his beer and poured him a shot.

"Do you know where he lives?"

"No, I don't want to."

Just then, a small group came into the bar. Chick would have to start tending and stop investigating for a while. "Make sure you keep me posted. Text me if you get anywhere." They said as they walked toward the group.

Chapter 20 - Middle-Aged Party Monsters

The group entering the bar was growing quickly. Chick had forgotten that there was some old popular band playing tonight, some acronym like M.O.D or M.D.C or S.O.L or S.O.F.B (some other fucking band). This was one of those nights that brought out a pile of the old punk rock dudes. They hadn't realized how late it was. Big Joe was here to work the door, and the floor was semi-crowded. Punk Billy was already starting to skank around the place and offend anybody in his vicinity.

"What ya having." Asked Chick.

"3 PBR's"

"Got it"

"3 PBR's"

"Got it"

Chick had a ton of acquaintances who thought they were their friend. They really only hung out with their fellow bartenders, and that was usually only after close. They would crew up sometimes for breakfast or lunch and hang out during the day. Evenings weren't easy because they were always working opposite shifts. Beyond this, Chick was mostly a loner and an introvert. For them, this investigation was exciting, and it felt good for Chick to want to interact and engage with people.

Gus and Stacia were still talking at the end of the bar. Chick wanted terribly to know what they were saying. They kept glancing over at them, trying to make out the mood.

The first band started playing. It was the local band 'Bloody Backpacks,' who hammered out 30-second gut punches without breaks. Chick always thought it was so odd that these old dudes could push each other around, in Doc Martens, with minor casualties, on what essentially became an ice rink of spilled beer. When one did go down, it was probably the massive amount of padding in their flight jacket that rebounded them back up to their feet or maybe it was their fellow participants re-enacting the battle of Bunker Hill, where no man shall be left on the floor.

Chick was moving fast tonight. Their mind was on the investigation. They couldn't wait to get back to it. Something about solving this thing made their heart pound. They took an opportunity as the next band started playing to move outside for a smoke. This would also allow them to check on the bike situation. They moved back to the end of the bar.

"Hey Stacia, Gus!"

"What's up?" Stacia yelled over the music.

"Going out for a smoke."

Stacia threw a thumbs up.

"Hey Brit, I'm going to grab a smoke." Chick shouted to their fellow bartender.

"Got it, Rae" Brit shouted back while pouring half a Red Bull into a shaker. Chick's name was actually Rachel.

The three pushed their way to the door and exited the venue. There was a swarm of punks standing around the sidewalk smoking and reminding each other, with very slurred speech, of this time or that time that this happened or that happened. "GG Allen, Suicidal Tendencies, Negative Approach and The Krabs. Punched a guy, got slammed, was homeless and we'll always miss him." "You want a hit?" "I'm good." "Remember so and so?" "Yeah man, too bad."

Chick led the gang over near Jake's bike. The three stared at it and each lit a solemn and inquisitive cigarette. Gus was getting tired, a little more irritable than usual and a little more broken. "Shit!" he yelled. "Lily's cats!"

"I've got to go feed and water them. Fuck!"

"Dude, go feed the cats and do what you gotta do! Stacia and I will keep an eye out for Jake and try to watch the bike," Chick said, offering as a solution.

"Yeah, are you sure?"

Stacia, "yeah, of course, go feed the cats! Who knows, maybe she's at home!"

"Okay, okay"

Gus headed back to his car at Stacia's place. He was anxious to be back at Lily's. If she wasn't there, him being there would help him feel closer to her in some ways. While Gus was crossing the street a couple of punks wandered over to Chick and Stacia and offered them a hit off a bowl.

"I'm cool, man," said Chick.

"Yeah, cool, I'll take a hit," replied Stacia. She could use it.

"Cool bike." said one of the dudes.

"It is." said Chick as though they were just there to admire the Harley.

"Jake's bike." said the same dude. "That dudes fucked up. Stay away from that guy."

"Oh yeah? Why's that?" Stacia said.

"Dudes a real psycho, man." the other dude chimed in with an almost Irish accent, an accent he most likely acquired while drinking. "He's got some kind of sick fucking hatred toward women. I mean, a lot of guys hate women, but Jake likes to take ownership of women he doesn't even know. He'll stalk and harass them in weird little ways. Like, if he was gonna cut you with a knife, Jake the guy who'd choose to stab you just a little, with the tip, once a week until you were full of bloody fucking little holes. He'd definitely do it that way, instead of just stabbing you, full on, like a real man." his accent grew thicker the longer he spoke.

Chick smiled, "fucking Jesus."

"Yup." The other dude kind of chuckled and coughed at the same time as the smoke excited his lungs. "Fuck that guy, ha-huh-guh."

A guy pulled up on a black Harley-Davidson Road King Classic. Got off the bike, smiled, shook hands and half hugged the two dudes. He headed into the bar. Chick spotted a decal on the saddle bag.

"I hate that fucking dynaflo." Chick read out loud, "hey, I know that guy."

"Fuck that guy too ha-ha-huh-gah-guh." the dude with the bowl said with a smile.

"You think he knows Jake?" said Chick.

"Naw. maybe? dunno."

Chapter 21 - Love Cats

Gus just arrived at his car and spotted Roger in his usual spot. He decided to walk over, give Roger a pet, and eye up the house. "Cock sucker," Gus voiced. There were no lights on, and nobody appeared to be around. He walked up near the porch, but it was dark, and he didn't feel like he'd make any progress poking around, so he turned and walked back toward his car. It was true that having Chick and Stacia team up with him helped ease his nerves. This was evident in the sudden fear and rage that was running from his toes up to his clenched fists. He slammed the side of that fist on the dashboard, grunting out, "fuck, fuck, fuck." His fist made a small crack and indentation in the brittle dashboard vinyl. The bobblehead dog on his dashboard was nodding along to the violence. Gus flicked the knob on the radio releasing "Interstate Love Song" throughout the car. He fell back in his seat, put down his armrest, grabbed a smoke out of his pack of smokes and lit one. Cigarette gripped tight between his front teeth, he put the car into drive, pressed the gas pedal in defeat and headed away. He glanced at Roger in his rearview. It was at that moment that he realized that he and Roger were both left out in the cold. He slammed the car in reverse, looking over his shoulder with the cigarette still tight between his teeth. He slammed on the brakes next to the doghouse, jumped out of the car, gave Roger a look and raised his eyebrows. He bent over and unhooked Roger's lead. Roger just sat, waiting for a sign from Gus regarding next moves. Gus walked over to the front door and looked back at Roger. Roger just stared back at him. "Well, are you coming?" Gus waved his hand toward the front door. Roger took no time, rather was a bolt of lightning from his saucer-shaped hole in the dirt to the front seat of that car. "Slide over," Gus said as he joined Roger in the front seat, put the car back into drive, and spun the tires out of there. He looked at Roger, and Roger looked back at him. "Fuck those guys," Gus said out loud. This time, he wasn't talking to himself; he was talking to Roger.

Gus and Roger were rolling through a rather hoppin' strip of the city. Several bars and hipster restaurants, breweries, and cideries. It was hard to drive down this road on any given evening. "They might as well close the damn street." Gus waved his hand around while Roger, sitting upright in his seat, took everything in. "Here is where everyone goes, Roger. Young hipsters, old yuppies, middle-aged 'fabulous' types. They all come here. It's safe here. None of the people here are revolutionary, and none of them have anything to say. They just want to shine bright like a diamond with all the other fucking diamonds. It's an adult prep school, and the walls protecting the campus are so far away from the buildings that its residents have the illusion of freedom. There is, in fact, no freedom here. If anybody in these groups acted out of line, it would destroy the illusion and would be promptly extinguished. If anybody in this group didn't conform, it would imply there weren't rules. Sure, they dress differently - mods, punks, yacht-looking guys, golf clothes guys, motorcycle gents - but it's all just different shades of lipstick on napkins. The appearance of being sexy while being… a Kleenex." Gus smiled at Roger. It was fun to talk to somebody. Roger actually seemed interested in the conversation too, glancing over at Gus every so often while admiring the lights and movements along the streets.

Gus pulled a left at Division and was a couple of blocks from Lily's place. He stopped at the Dollar store and quickly ran in to grab a bag of dog food and a treat for Roger. He locked the car and left it running. He ran in, grabbed a leash, some food, a dog treat that looked like a poop emoji, and a Monster Mocha for himself. "Fucking Lily got me on this shit," he mumbled to himself. "Poop emoji, dope," said the clerk as he rang up the stuff. Gus glanced out to Roger still perched upright in his seat, looking around. Gus gave the clerk money and went back to the car.

"Hey man." Gus glanced over his shoulder. "You got any change or a cigarette?"

Gus got in his car, back up and drove out the parking lot. "Nope." Gus said to Roger with a smirk. Roger didn't say anything back.

"Here we are." Said Gus as they pulled into Lily's.

He put the car in park and pulled the bag from the

store out of the back seat. "Here we go, boy." He reached over to put the leash on Roger. Roger squinted and pulled back a little. He wasn't into it. Gus whispered that it was okay and gently reached around to clasp the leash. Roger complied. Gus opened the door and gave Roger a quiet "Here, boy" and Roger flopped out of the car onto the dirt. Gus grabbed the other bag from the back, and the two let themselves into Lily's apartment. Mulder and Scully both came up and started rubbing on Gus's legs. Roger was cool and began to sniff each cat's backside. "What is that a greeting?" asked Gus. The cats were hungry and anxious for affection. He put some food in each of their bowls and filled up their water bowl with fresh water. Roger quickly pranced over to the water and helped himself. Gus grabbed another bowl from the pantry, opened up Roger's bag, and poured some dog food. Roger quickly shifted from the water bowl to the food bowl. Gus replenished the water bowl while asking the cats how they were doing. They were eating and didn't respond. Gus decided to sit for a minute while the cats and the dog ate and thought about Lily. His eyes were weary, and the fact that the apartment hadn't changed at all was a huge letdown. He popped a beer he had grabbed from the fridge, and Roger joined him on the couch. "Where is she, Roger? What am I gonna do?" Roger looked at Gus again as if he understood. Gus texted Stacia, "Anything with the bike???" and flipped on the TV. "Criminal Minds" was on. Criminal Minds was always on. His phone chirped, it was Stacia, "Nothing yet, man. Bike's still here."

"Okay," and he sat back again on the couch. The dog finally started to get comfortable, and the cats were purring next to his head.

He would shut his eyes… just for a minute.

Chapter 22 - Scully and Mulder

The voice of a dog barking grew more and more near as Gus opened his eyes. He quickly squinted as the light became too bright to look at. It took him a second to realize that it was Roger that he heard barking, but the sound was still pretty distant. He stood up from the couch, and everything around him was a blanket of light and white that could only be described as a scene from *THX 1138* or the Jupiter scene in *2001: A Space Odyssey*. He put his arm up over his eyes and began walking toward what he could barely make out as the television screen. He made out the shape of a woman in the washed-out colors emitting from the LEDs.

"Lily?" he said with a quiet whisper. The light enveloped him. He assumed he was dying as those near death have so many times described this scene. He felt weightless. He heard a voice, distant like the dog's bark, that was absolutely the voice of Morgan Freeman. The voice said, "There is nothing here for you, Gus."

"What?"

"There is nothing here for you, my boy," replied the voice.

"What do you mean there is nothing here for me," asked Gus, still squinting from the light of the whitewashed horizon.

"Gus, there is, unfortunately, nothing here."

"What the fuck is going on? Where am I? Am I dead?"

"You're neither dead nor alive. There is nothing here, Gus." said Morgan Freeman's voice.

Gus started walking in the direction he thought the voice was coming from. He suddenly felt pressure on his body like he was moving through air very quickly.

"I'll show you something," said the voice from what now sounded just inches from Gus's ear.

"But you said there was nothing here," said Gus as though his words were written for him.

"Nothing can't be nothing without something," said Morgan Freeman's voice, "I'll show you."

Appearing, still washed out by the light, he could make out large square blocks emitting their own light, but this light was yellow. The image seemed familiar. He couldn't hear Roger anymore.

Morgan Freeman's voice, once more, from what sounded like it came from behind the golden cubes, refrained, "There is nothing here, Gus. No matter how much of something there might seem to be here, there is, in fact, nothing here."

Then the voice asked, "Gus, would you by chance have a cigarette?"

"What the fuck, Morgan Freeman?"

The familiar yellow cubes started to fade into the distance at an increasing rate. Gus could hear Roger barking again. Suddenly it felt like the floor gave out from under him and he was falling through the light. He could make out some of the shapes and colors of the city below. He fell faster and faster until he felt himself go into shock.

"Yes indeed, there is nothing here."

Chapter 23 - Desert Hills

Lily awoke with that feeling you only get, on occasion, when you are in an unfamiliar place. The feeling of being barely conscious while out-of-focus abnormal smells, sounds, and surroundings enter your senses. She first caught the blink of the smoke detector out of the corner of her eye. The blinking light was also reflected in the vanity mirror. The bed had the wobble that antique budget motel beds always have. The hum of her little retro fridge reminded her where she was. She shuffled over and out of the sheets, sat upright on the side of the bed, and took a swig from her coke. As she set down her drink, she glanced at the clock. "7:00 AM. Damn." She realized that this was a good and much-needed sleep. She stood up and threw on a pair of sweats she had bought at Target. She pulled a cigarette from her pack and picked up her lighter and opened the door to a brightly filled void. Her eyes adjusted, and she stepped into the light. She felt the warm air and sun hit her as she lit her first cigarette of the day. An older black man with a slight limp and a cane was walking by. "Could I bother you for a cigarette?" he had a voice like Morgan Freeman. "Sure, one second," Lily opened her door and reached in for her pack. She removed a smoke and handed it to him.

"What brings you to the Desert Hills?" asked the

man while lighting his cigarette. "Just passing through," exclaimed Lily.

"Oh, yes, passing through. So many people are always passing through," he said, "it's as though there is nothing here," he chuckled a little and started shuffling along. "Yes, yes," he continued as he walked away.

Lily took a few more slow drags off the cigarette while admiring the look of the Desert Hills sign and old Chevy parked in front of it.

"I guess I'll go get nothing to eat," she spoke out loud imitating a deep velvet voice.

She walked down past the Chevy to the entrance to the parking lot and surveyed her surroundings. There were, what appeared to be, a string of businesses that identify as either very American or of very Route 66 heritage. She couldn't see anything that looked like breakfast, so she decided to hop around the weird outside pedestal sink and into the lobby to inquire.

"Tally's," said the woman, "It's a few blocks up the street, just past the antique stores and the wall of America," She smiled.

"Thanks," said Lily who just as quickly exited the lobby.

She stepped back out onto the street and glanced in the direction the woman was pointing. She could see the antique mall and decided she should walk. She went back to her room and grabbed her backpack and her sunglasses and headed out to "Tally's" just past the "Wall of America."

Lily loved the air right now. It was the right amount of warm and dry. She liked the brightness of the sun on her back and the blue sky up ahead. "Antique Mall - Route 66." She had to admit to herself that she loved the crudely painted Route 66 sign. She liked that it was crude more than anything it represented. It had a folk-art vibe which she dug. She walked slowly past the antique store, eyeing up as much as she could in the windows as she strolled. She saw an old lamp that her grandmother had and a set of dishes that they ate off of when she was a kid. She paused here and lit another smoke. Lily was sentimental in the strangest way. She found items like this to be so fascinating, almost excited that she got to be in that moment with those objects. At the same time, she had a certain hatred for her childhood. She was every bit as independent as a child as she is as an adult and was equally never comfortable in her surroundings. That's why it's odd seeing her become sentimental toward these objects. Her time with them, even as a young person, was fleeting. They were things she wanted to escape from. Being here, with these objects is more of a reminder of what she escaped rather than what was comforting.

She crossed the street at the end of the store. After a few more blocks of businesses that are in every town, everywhere in America, she spotted a wall with another crude, but better Route 66 sign painted on it followed by a really nice painting of the word "Illinois" as it would have appeared on one of those old "welcome to Illinois" postcards. Missouri, Kansas… She could see Tally's up ahead. She tossed her cigarette into "America's Main

Street" and crossed the road. She glanced up at the Historic Route 66 and E 11th Street signs standing tall in front of the neon-lit "Tally's on Route 66."

"Dammit, no phone."

She took a picture with her eyes.

Chapter 24 - There Is Nothing Here

Gus's eyes burst wide open as he sat upright, as though he had been pulled by the gravity of a black hole. He looked at the TV, which was now airing an episode of Cold Case. He was still a little shaken up. He grabbed his smokes and lit one, glancing over at Roger, who was laid up on the other side of the couch and staring at him. He walked into the kitchen and started some coffee.

"Fuck was that, Roger? There is nothing here? That shit was real, man. Like really real." He could still hear Morgan Freeman's voice in his head, clear as a bell. "Did you see any of that, Roger? Where the fuck were you, dude?" Roger's ears perked up as he intently listened to Gus.

"Oh shit! Hey Roger, check this out!" Gus grabbed the emoji bone he bought at the store, "here you go, my man!" Roger gently sniffed and took the bone from Gus's hand, then took it casually into the living room.

Gus remembered every bit of his dream so vividly. The strangely familiar glowing yellow cubes. They were so familiar, but he couldn't seem to make the connection. He didn't want to fall asleep and realized he needed to check his phone and get back in on the investigation. He just felt so good being at Lily's, making coffee while enjoying the occasional smell of her scents drifting off of things - the candles, scarves, and cats. She had an old poster from the movie *Léon: The Professional* which he loved to stare at. He could somehow get lost in Jean Reno's sunglasses, his face, and the face of young Natalie Portman.

"A perfect assassin. An innocent girl. They have nothing left to lose except each other."

He decided to write Lily a note, a letter, a love letter.

"My love for you takes on different shapes and forms in each moment. It evolves with each and every expression, conversation, and experience. Sometimes I don't like you, and sometimes I really like you. Sometimes I hate you, and sometimes you hate me. Sometimes we love to hate, and other times we hate to love. You are an enigma, child. You are a lost child. Even in the grasp of evil, when the thought of stabbing out your eyes crosses my mind, your face, the very portrait of the innocent woman inside, tears at my heart, pushes me into a comfort and warmth that can only be explained as true love. The shapes and forms that are the roadmap of our long but somehow fast road toward senior citizens, I look to your face, through your eyes and into your soul, to guide me to the end with strength and understanding. Fuck you, Lily. Right now, I hate you. I see your face now in everything around me. It kills me to know that I understand you, and it kills me more that I don't know what the fuck is going on."

"Fuck, Roger, I have to work today!"

Roger glanced up at Gus. He was probably wondering if there was another treat.

"I should just call in sick or quit. I mean, is this reason enough to take a day? I don't know man; I feel like I should probably just go. I don't wanna put people out, you know?"

Roger stood up in anticipation for a bone.

Gus wandered into the bathroom to take a leak and a shower. While he was standing over the toilet, he thought about how odd it was that all of Lily's stuff was still here - everything from her toothbrush to her contact lens kit. One of the cats, Mulder, jumped up onto the sink and waited for Gus to turn on the faucet. He nuzzled it and looked up at Gus in anticipation. He was fully aware of Mulder's love for tap water. Gus turned the faucet on a quarter turn and gave Mulder a fist bump on his head. Mulder dipped his head under the stream of water and took a taste. From there he took full-on tongue fulls of water. "Fucking Mulder," Gus chuckled.

Gus jumped into the shower. The water felt good as he scrubbed himself with Lil's body wash and loofa. He placed his forehead onto the tile and let the water run down and over the tattoos on his back. As he exited the shower, he caught a familiar site out of the corner of his eye. It was a photograph Lily had framed and put in her bathroom. It was a black and white photo, in the style of Jason Lee, of a desert landscape with the Waffle House sign towering above the horizon, the only thing in color. He immediately connected this to his Morgan Freeman dream,

"There is nothing here, my boy."

Chapter 25 - Coffee III

Stacia and Chick had been inquiring about Jake all night. At this point, both were a little drunk, a little loose. While investigating, they were also flirting and enjoying each other's company. A second band went on, then a third. The old punks started to dissipate, and those still on the floor were starting to slow down. There were a lot of glazed eyes and macho hugs going around the room. Between flirting with Stacia, pulling PBR's from the cooler, and collecting tips, Chick was starting to clean up. The third band wound down to a crowd about half the size of the group that had previously shaken the place. Punk Bill was now barely upright, staring at one of the speakers monitors and talking to it with some kind of Billy Idol accent.

"Last Call!" Shouted Brit.

Punk Bill raised both of his half empty cans of PBR into the air, lowered his head, and let out a slurred "Oi!" He was watching the band tearing down their gear, directing them loosely as though he were a tarmac guide, and his cans of beer were his orange batons.

Stacia sat at the bar while Chick and Brit started wiping everything down. There were still about 10 people in the bar and four of them were staff. Brit poured Big Joe and Clark, the sound guy, a shot of Jameson. She then wandered over to Stacia and Chick and poured the three of them a shot. The three lifted their glasses, tapped them on the bar, and swallowed them down. Brit poured a little water into one of the shot glasses and lit a smoke. Chick followed suit.

"So, what's going on with you guys?" Brit asked as she poured them each a beer.

"Our friend is missing, and we aren't sure," Stacia looked at Brit.

"Stacia and her friend Lily were here last night, and after Lily took some shit from Jake, she just sort of left and didn't say anything. We found out later that Jake tried to hold up the liquor store, got himself pretty beat up and ended up at my neighbor's house. We are concerned that Jake or my neighbor Jesse have something to do with it. We don't know. Her phone is off, her car is gone, and Gus is freaking out," explained Chick.

"Gus, who was here earlier?" asked Brit. "What if he had something to do with it? "It seems like it's always the guy that has something to do with it. Is he a freak?"

Stacia started laughing and even snorted a little bit. "Yes, he's a freak ha-ha! He's not that kind of freak. He loves her and is absolutely going fucking nuts over her being gone."

Brit poured them another shot and exclaimed, "Yeah, he's a freak who loves her, sounds about right to me." She took her shot.

Brit had a tough exterior that hinted at a difficult upbringing. It seemed like she had to raise herself and grow up fast, as they say. But despite the hardships, she reached a point in life where she was mostly content. She worked hard at her steady job and didn't fret too much about what she lacked. It was hard to dislike her, as nobody had a reason to.

"What about you two?" Brit nudged. "You have a little thing going on?"

Stacia and Chick looked at each other and smiled. Chick was blushing hard."

"Ahhh ha-ha, love is in the air," Brit exclaimed, grinning wider. "Come on, you two, let's close this place up and get out of here so you can get your freak on." Stacia and Chick blushed, looking embarrassed by the comment.

As they made their way out, Chick and Stacia stole a glance at the bike one last time. It still sat motionless.

"Stacia, how about we go to Black Hole?" Chick asked, referring to the same coffee shop where Gus had been earlier that morning.

"Sure!" Stacia replied.

"Let's walk over there. The weather is so nice," Chick suggested.

"Cool," Stacia agreed."

The coffee shop was buzzing with people considering it was 2:30 AM. It wasn't loaded with drunks like you might think. Mostly college age kids hanging out. What appeared dark and kind of dreary in the mornings was somehow bright and exciting at night. Stacia and Chick both ordered americanos to go. As they turned to leave, they noticed the neighbor Jesse, wearing a battered, old clash t-shirt partly covered by the black & white keffiyeh around his neck, sitting in the corner by the door. He definitely noticed them.

They tried to sneak by, but he didn't hesitate to ask them, "What the fuck did you two do with my dog?"

Stacia, "What the fuck are you talking about? Roger? I mean, Tank?"

"Yes, fucking Tank. He's gone, what the fuck did you do?"

"Look man, fuck off!" Chick was fired up and pissed.

"Fuck you, you fucking creepy, weird, fucking, whatever you are."

Chick made a fist and shakingly put it inches from Jesse's stone and leather face.

"We don't know where your dog is, man. Settle the fuck down," said Stacia with the authority of someone's mother or that of a recess attendant in grade school.

"Yeah, and while we are having a conversation why don't you tell us what the fuck your pal Jake did with our friend Lilly? Mother fucker." Chick was still in his face.

"What the fuck are you bitches or whatever talking about? I don't know anything about any Lily. What the fuck does that asshole Jake have to do with anything? You think that mother fucker took Tank? Sit the fuck down."

"We're good." Chick said.

"Look man, the night your pal Jake tried to rob the

liquor store he had also threw a pass at our friend Lily. Nobody has seen her since. That dude's bike is still parked at the bar, and we have some fucking questions for him. You dig, asshole?"

He looked up at Stacia and said, "what the fuck are you talking about? He ain't my pal and after he tried to rob the liquor store he stumbled up to my house with a massive gash on his head and a fucking serious gash in his gut. I did what I could to patch him up and help him sleep off his drunk bullshit. He stumbled around the next day like a damn fool. I thought he had a concussion or something, so I ran him to the ER. I left the mother fucker there and went home. That's the last I seen of that prick. Now, let's get back to real business. Where the fuck is my dog?" Jesse lit a cigarette at his table. The barista quickly jutted around tables, chairs, and people and intercepted.

"Man, what the fuck? Put that out!"

"Yeah, fuck, okay."

Jesse wobbled up and said to Chick and Stacia. "Remember, I know you have something to do with Tank. Get the fuck out of my way," as he limped out the door.

Stacia and Chick sat down to recover from the encounter and work off a little of their buzz. "You guys were talking about Lily," said the barista. "Gus, I think, was in here this morning looking for her. She's in here all the time. What's going on? Like, I swear to god that if I was missing for two days or even a week the only people who would notice would be the owners of this place. Seriously, like, nobody would look for me. My cats wouldn't even look for me…"

While our barista friend explains this to basically everyone in the place, Stacia text Gus,

"What up man, we just had a run in with my neighbor Jesse. Dude is missing his dog. Says he brought Jake to the ER that night."

"WTF?"

"…not even my mom would look for me."

"Okay, okay," Chick cut him off. "We gotta go. Common Stacia, let's go."

The two headed outside and lit cigarettes. It was quiet outside of the coffee shop. The air smelled good at 3:30AM. The coffee helped clear their heads. They started walking back toward Stacia's place.

"Nothing from Gus yet."

"Hopefully we don't lose him too."

"Right? Between Lily, the dog, this guy Jake. It's too much! ha-ha."

"We aren't also missing, right?" asked Chick.

"Maybe. Who knows?"

"Yup, no Roger," Stacia said as they walked past his doghouse and into the apartment.

Chapter 26 - Sir, You Know I Can't Give Out That Information.

Gus, in the living room, put on his jeans and sat back down on the couch. He remembered that he hadn't checked his phone. There were a couple text messages from Stacia. He looked at Roger, "my boy, you appear to have gone missing." Gus smiled a little.

"I'm sorry, Stacia."

"I snatched Roger and he's here at Lily's with me and the cats."

"After I fed everyone, I sat down and fell asleep."

"I'm going to check the hospital."

"I have to work today."

"Hmu"

Gus looked at Roger who had been staring at him for a while. "What's up dude, you need to go outside or something? We better get that out of the way." Roger stood up, ready to go. Gus put the leash on him and brought him outside. "Did you ever wonder, Roger, why the fuck your previous owner leaves you outside all the time? What makes somebody that fucking cruel, Roger? I mean, why didn't you tear his fucking hand off or something?" Roger squatted down in a bare patch of lawn and embarrassingly looked up at Gus. "I'm going to split for a little bit, Roger, unless you wanna go for a ride." Roger's ears sprang up and he began to pant with what Gus could only make out as a yes. They shuffled back into the apartment, retrieved Gus's keys, smokes, and wallet, and headed back out. Roger jumped up and down with excitement at the door of the car, ready to go!

Gus turned her over, backed up and out. He rolled out of the apartment and down the street toward the hospital area. It was one of those easy-like-a-Sunday-morning folks mixed with the movers and shakers kind of days. It was hard to navigate on days like this - slow-moving and patient cars pitted up against angsty, impatient cars. There was little room for an in-between guy like Gus. He liked to be able to light a smoke while driving and not have to worry about slamming into the car in front of him or being derailed by an asshole who's in a hurry. For such a simple act as driving, it pissed him off that you had to be so fucking attentive. They battled their way toward the hospital zone. "I don't know what to do with you when I go in," Gus said to Roger. "Do I just leave you in the car or what?" Gus pulled into a parking spot and cracked the passenger side window an inch or so. "I'll be right back, buddy," he said. Roger looked content with it.

Gus headed up the steep ramp to the hospital doors. He wandered up to the reception area where he smiled at the not-so-enthusiastic receptionist.

"I'm looking for my friend who I think was brought here," he said with a paired down version of his usual politeness.

"Name?" she asked.

"Jake Tomachewski," he replied.

She started typing into her computer. "When did we receive him?" she asked. "Couple of nights ago."

"He was released yesterday."

"Shoot," said Gus, "Do you have an address?" He thought his charm might get this one answered.

"Sir, you know I can't give out that kind of information." She was not enthused by his request at all.

"Are you sure? I mean, I need to make sure he's okay. We were pretty worried about his head wound."

"Sorry sir. I can't help you." She began shuffling papers around signaling to Gus that it was time for him to leave.

Gus went back to the car disappointed. He really was hoping he was onto something. It was obvious to Gus that perhaps this guy Jake had nothing to do with Lily's disappearance, but he was the last person to speak with her. There had to be a connection between her disappearance and this asshole. The irony of the two of them being impossible to find was enough to make him important. There were no leads on Lily but there were leads on Jake. Either way, the sting of it all was hard. Gus could put it away when on a mission but there were times that he was crippled. It was like all the blood in all of his veins became stiff and full of fire. He could feel his heart palpitate and eyes hurt. He'd feel dehydrated and sore everywhere. His hands were shaking while he had this panic attack. He struggled to get his keys into his car door. Roger was looking at him, tongue hanging out as he breathed. The rhythm of Roger put Gus right. He sat in the car and stared, unfocused, at bits of dirt on his windshield. He took a minute to regroup. He didn't want to let any memories flood him with emotions. He had to work today and had some shit to do until then.

He started the car.

Chapter 27 - El Rancho Grande

Tally's was 100% a cliché of Americana. The restaurant was flooded with neon, red vinyl, and aluminum. It was like Route 66 went to a retro party, got drunk on peppermint schnapps and puked this thing up. It wasn't really the Route 66 Lily admired in books, photography, and movies. It wasn't pure like a lot of the wrecked diners and motels along the highway. This was more of a glamor shot from the mall or an amusement park for Route 66 fans. It was a remake of an old movie with modern equipment but poor acting. The staff, also washed in red, were pleasant as she was seated in one of the big, clumsy booths. As she gazed at her reflection in the blank screen of her phone, she realized that she needed a new one for research purposes. She wanted to investigate the places she visited or planned to go, without drawing attention to her whereabouts or being sidetracked by others' needs. She knew that this could make her appear selfish, and she acknowledged it. This type of selfishness stemmed from both a defense mechanism to avoid getting hurt and from being selfless for a prolonged period, which resulted in her rebellious act. As soon as the idea of getting a new phone occurred to her, she became restless. She quickly finished her meal, so she could hurry to a store to buy one. Although she hated being held captive by her need for a new device, she was powerless to change it.

"Where can I get a phone?" she asked her server.

"I dunno, maybe just head up toward the highway. I think there are a few cell phone stores along Admiral."

"Thanks," said Lily while putting cash down on the table.

After leaving Tally's, Lily began walking toward her hotel. The street was lined with car dealerships, mechanic shops, and antique stores as far as she could see. When she arrived at the Desert Hills, she walked straight to her car. She started it up while the warmth of the sun on the front seat enveloped her. She left the parking lot and drove back toward Tally's, heading north until she crossed over the highway and saw Admiral Pl. Lily took a right turn. "This was modern America," she said to herself. Arby's, Burger King, Advance Auto. After a few blocks she saw a T-Mobile sign and pulled into the parking lot. Upon exiting the car, she heard the usual cat calls from some cabrones hanging out in the parking lot. "Vete a la mierda, cabrones!" she yelled to them. These guys started laughing and took this gesture as an invite.

"You sound like you could use a little help with your Spanish. Why don't you let me teach you a lesson?" said the cabrón with the bowling shirt as the three walked toward her.

"Fuck you, man," replied Lily in a calm way.

"Sounds like you also need to learn some manners," the bowling shirt cabrónsaid.

"What the fuck? Are these guys reading this shit

from a fucking really bad movie script?" Lily thought to herself. T-shirt cabrón put his hand on the roof of her car while bowling shirt cabrón did the same but on the opposite side of her. He was in her face.

"Why don't we get down to lesson number one," he said just inches from her face.

With lightning speed, Lily pulled out a small knife and stabbed the man in the abdomen three or four times before shoving him out of her way. The other two men were startled by the suddenness of the attack. Lily made a run for the cell phone store and dashed inside. From the window, she watched as the two men helped their injured amigo, Bowling Shirt, into their car before speeding off. It was clear that they were not expecting any violence, and Lily knew that they were only playing a role. "I bet his mom will not be fucking thrilled about this," she thought to herself. The man at the counter said, "Ma'am, can I help you?"

"Me? Yeah. Him? Not so much. I need a cellphone."

"Sure thing, did you want a plan or pay as you go?"

"Pay as you go, please. iPhone."

"Sure, we've got a pretty good deal right now."

"Okay, yeah, whatever. Ring it up."

As she left the store, she noticed a trail of blood drops on the ground. She was surprised by her own actions and shaken up by what had just happened. She needed a moment to compose herself and figure out what to do next. Lily decided to find a nearby place to have a quick drink and set up her new phone. Her hands were trembling with adrenaline. She knew that this was something she would never have done back home. Lily realized there was a stark difference between her home persona and her traveling persona. At home, she was familiar with the people and places around her and knew what to expect. However, while traveling, she felt more vulnerable and alone. Although this feeling was not unique to any particular place in America, the unfamiliarity of it all made her more uncertain. When the guy threatened her personal space, Lily acted on an instinct she hadn't felt in a while. The knife she used was a small pocketknife, so he'd be okay. "Maybe next time the motherfucker will think twice before acting like a fucking moron," she thought to herself.

Lily got into her car and drove south towards Route 66. She decided that if she was going to have a drink this early in the day, it might as well be on The Mother Road. Lily navigated through a maze of urban homes, all 1950s-style brick ranch houses that seemed to stretch on forever. Everything still had the hangover of winter to it. She drove through what looked like a massive park, getting turned around several times before finally finding herself back on the Mother Road. Home base. Continuing down Route 66, she scanned for bars but none of them looked open. She was slightly startled as the car belonging to the Cabrones from the cell phone store was crossing the intersection in front of her. She made note of the hospital buildings to her left. "For fuck's sake," she muttered under her breath.

She spotted a place called El Rancho Grande just past the hospital.

"Tequila it is," she pulled into the parking lot hard. This place had its very own, very neon sign. Walking in, it appeared as cliche as the Mexicans that were fucking with her at the cell phone store. They did have a bar, a pretty nice little bar, where Lily planted herself.

"Dos tequilas, Por Favor," Lily had been working on her Spanish a little over a year and was terrible at it.

"Si, coming right up," replied the bartender. "Anything else? Menu?"

"No menu, a coke please," she said.

"Dos tequilas y Coke back. Coming right up, Chica!"

The bartender was a handsome young guy with a lot of charm. He was dressed as a bartender should dress with a clean and pressed black shirt and a gold name tag that read Miguel.

"What brings you in?" he asked.

"I just stabbed a guy a bunch and need a few minutes to unwind," she said as seriously as she could to Miguel.

"ha-ha, You're a badass hey?" Miguel didn't take her seriously.

"You could say I'm the baddest of all the badasses around. I'm actually just on the road and am taking a pit stop."

"Where are you from?"

"Michigan."

"Detroit Tigers!"

"Yup, Detroit Tigers."

"Cool. Let me know if you need another round," he said.

She placed the phone's box on the bar and quickly wiped off her knife blade with a napkin before heading to the restroom to dispose of it. After washing her hands, she returned to the bar and opened the box. Within a few minutes, she had the phone set up and running. She opened Google Maps and located her current position. Looking at the routes to Mexico, she identified San Antonio as a good 8-hour drive from Tulsa and decided it would be her next destination. Despite what she's heard about Texas, having never been there and hearing nothing that made her want to visit, she figured it was as good a place as any to explore.

"You want another shot, señorita?"

"Thanks Miguel, two more."

"Two more it is!" he twirled the bottle through the air, "The Mother Road," he stated. "Where are you staying?"

"Desert Hills"

"Cool place."

"It has its charm," She said, "and no, you can't check out my room," she smiled.

Miguel laughed and poured them each a shot. "Salud!" and they both drank.

"It's been fun, Miguel, but I must be on my way," she said as though an elegant patron was speaking through her.

"Good meeting you too, chica. Come back later for mariachi."

"Maybe."

She grabbed the phone box and her backpack. The light outside hit her like a brick to the face. She liked this air. She headed back to Desert Hills.

"Maybe it was time to leave Tulsa."

She unlocked her door, walked into the room, and turned on the TV. Sitting down on the bed with a half-empty bottle of Coke, she saw that "Cold Case" was on. "God, I hope Scully and Mulder are okay," she thought to herself, "dos gatos!"

Chapter 28 - Harley Davidson

Chick had spent another night at Stacia's place, and neither of them had to work, so they got up, ready to continue the investigation between the flirting, wrestling, and touching that comes with budding romance. Chick was really pretty. They had all the features of a classic beauty: big, beautiful eyes, luscious lips, soft perfect skin, soft brown hair cut short, and a cute little nose ring. They had quite a few tattoos of various things, mostly old school sailor type of tattoos: a hula girl, skulls, Bettie Page, a swallow, that kinda stuff. Stacia thought this was so cool. She loved fucking Chick. Chick had all the feminism and beauty of a true female while having an appendage that gave Stacia chills to her core. This morning, just like earlier this morning, Stacia felt a tingle thinking about it. She grabbed Chick's hand and batted at them with her long, natural lashes. She threw Chick onto the chair around the kitchen table and went down on them. Chick was warm with blood rushing all through their body, stretching their cock to near explosion. Stacia sat on Chick's lap, and they both came quickly, both flush red.

"How about some coffee," Chick smiled at Stacia with eyes that expressed an overwhelmed satisfaction."

"For sure!" Stacia pulled herself from Chick and bounced over toward the coffee maker. "Where should we start today?" she asked Chick.

"I dunno, let's check out the bike."

"Sounds like a plan, Stan," She giggled a little, cheeks still flush, hair all messy.

It was a very spring-like day as they walked toward the bar. The sun kissed both of their lust rushed faces. People were out and about, wearing earbuds, riding motorcycles without helmets, and cycling in spandex. Some people wore shorts or tights and large headphones, while others hung out on their porches smoking weed. Spring brought the thumping bass of cars, the smell of burning tires, and the sound of sirens. Birds were singing, and a guy was sitting on the sidewalk talking to a broken piece of bumper. Chick and Stacia both had made their coffee to go. They walked up to the Tip Top parking lot, but the motorcycle was gone.

"Fuck me."

"I just did."

"Hey Rae!" Larry's voice bellowed from the corner, "whatchya doing?!"

"Hey Larry, hey Paul, what are you guys doing?"

"It's a nice day," said Paul quietly and peacefully. "What are you guys doing?"

"We were just checking out the motorcycle that was here."

"OH YEAH, Jake JUSSSST LEFT!" Larry became really loud, "He took off on his HARRLLLLLLEYYYY DAAAVVIDDDSOOON!"

"Oh, shit, you guys know Jake?"

"Yeah," said Paul. "He's been around as long as us."

"AND HE HAS A HARRLLLLLEYYYY DAAAVVIDDDSOOON!"

"Yup, he has a Harley Davidson." Paul reinstated while Larry made the motions of twisting a throttle in the air.

"Do you guys know where he lives?" asked Stacia.

"Yup, he lives on our street," said Paul.

"YUP!" Nodded Larry.

"   W   h   e   r   e   ?   "

"43 INDIANA AVENUE!" Larry was proud to tell people his address. His mom made him memorize it in case of an emergency.

"You guys are the best!" exclaimed Chick.

"Thanks Rae, you're the best."

Stacia immediately text Gus,

"43 Indiana"

"Jake lives a couple houses down from there."

"I'm going to head that way now," Gus replied.

"We'll meet you there."

"Thanks Larry, thanks Paul!" They headed back to Stacia's to get her car.

Gus immediately headed in the direction of Indiana Avenue. Roger could feel the energy in the car and was panting with some excitement. As they approached Indiana Ave, he noticed Stacia's car approaching from the opposite direction. They met each other in the middle of the street and Gus rolled down his window.

"Roger!" yelled Stacia from the driver's seat. Chick raised and shook their hand at Gus. Roger stood a little taller and gave a quiet yelp toward Stacia.

"I can't believe you took Roger."

"I know, I know. It's actually been pretty natural having him with me. Where is this guy?"

"We gotta look for the bike. It should be this block. Why don't you pull over and ride with me and Roger."

The four of them navigated slowly up the block but there was no sign of a Harley. Chick did note to the group that the house on the corner had a Harley-Davidson blanket posing as a curtain in one of the upstairs windows. "That has to be it," said Stacia. "Alright, I'll drive through the alley," Gus whispered like someone in the house might hear him, "look for anything, please!" Gus grew even quieter.

As they rolled through the alley the sound of the gravel under the tires seemed incredibly loud along with the squeaking of the breaks. Everyone was silent including Roger who was also looking intently at the surroundings.

Chick, with a disappointed tone murmured, "I don't see anything."

About halfway down the alley, Gus sped up and turned the car around the corner, parking it on the street. "Stay here," he said as he jumped out and ran up to the house. He pulled the lid on the mailbox, grabbed a piece of mail, and ran back to the car.

"Patricia fucking Tomachewski."

Chick yelled, "Tomachewski! This must be it!"

"Yeah, but who the fuck is Patricia?"

"Probably his fucking mom," said Stacia.

Gus looked at his watch, "Shit, I gotta go to work. I gotta run Rodger back to Lily's. No matter how much I want to stay and pursue this, it'll really have to wait."

"No problem, Gus. We can keep digging a bit and we'll stop down to the bar to see you later."

"That'd be great, thanks guys."

"Bye Roger," Stacia and Chick said as they exited Gus's car.

Roger and Gus drove away, eyeing up the house and Stacia's car. Gus didn't feel like working at the bar, but he thought it would be a much-needed distraction after today. They drove calmly and stopped at the coffee shop, where Gus grabbed an americano and discovered the puppuccino. He brought them back to the car and watched as Roger quickly slurped his drink. Gus turned up the radio, and "Sunday Bloody Sunday" by U2 was playing. He turned it up even louder and took off.

Chapter 29 - $20 and a Pack of Smokes

Shortly after leaving Jake's house with Gus, Stacia and Chick decided to grab some coffee and chat. They headed to the Black Hole and ordered an Americano and a mocha, deciding to enjoy the beautiful day by sitting outside. They had those old iron tables that wobbled with some weight, and everything was chained up and bolted into the sidewalk. At the table on the other side of the entrance, there was a guy, probably in his late twenties, with a full beard. He was wearing a Scottish tam and a kilt and appeared to be talking to himself. As he spoke, he would glance over at Stacia and Chick, but not directly at them, more like he was looking through them. The words he was saying were mumbled and incomprehensible. Chick and Stacia both took a sip of their coffee. They knew Mr. Scotland to be a regular around here, so his presence didn't surprise them. They chose to ignore him because he had a tendency to direct his mumbling at anyone who provoked him. They also wanted to postpone his inevitable request for a cigarette. The table they were at sat in front of a window. The guy on the other side of the glass appeared to be working on a manuscript that used the word "fuck" a lot. He was typing in what appeared to be a 22pt font, so nobody had trouble making out the word over and over again. The gal on the other side of him was drawing and was really good. You'd catch these sketches of men and women draped over various things in Picasso-esque pencil nudes. The figures were either in pain or in ecstasy. "I know that feeling," Chick said with a wink while pointing at the artwork. Stacia's face lit up with a giant smile reflecting on the morning's filthy acts.

"What do you think?" Chick asked.

"About what, Lily?"

"No, about us, you, and me? This whole thing?"

Stacia became a little nervous, "I think this is fun, Chick. I really like you."

"Cool," Chick sort of hopped up and down in their chair smiling. "Tell me something about yourself. Anything." Chick said with ambition to grow their relationship.

Stacia wasn't very good at expressing herself in such a way. It took a long time for her to trust someone enough to start talking about herself in the way Chick was expecting. She reached across the table, took Chick's hand, and looked into their eyes. "Let's go see Gus at the bar," she said.

"Cool."

In the car, Stacia glanced down and noticed she was low on gas. They pulled into the little gas station under the overpass and up to the pump. They both went in. Josh, our attendant, smiled and asked, "How's it going?"

"Good, said Stacia."

Josh, the attendant, was ringing up a regular named Jimmy, who was playing the numbers. Jimmy turned and looked down at Stacia. "I'll be damned," he uttered in his cool, old guy shaft sort of way. "Look-ee here." He glanced up at Fernando on the other side of the tiny gas station, then back down at Stacia's breasts while lowering his glasses to the tip of his nose. Fernando was a small and very round Mexican who smiled, looked at Jimmy and after cupping his hands around his breasts said, "ahhh papayas." He and Jimmy both laughed while the attendant said, "Okay, stop it you guys."

Gus had dropped off Roger, fed and watered the pets, and hurried home to change and gather some things to take to Lily's place where he planned to stay indefinitely. Being around her things and her smells felt good, and the cats needed him.

After changing into fresh clothes, brushing his teeth, washing his face, and applying some cologne, he packed a duffle bag with a few changes of clothes, socks, and underwear. He also included his toiletries, grabbed his laptop, and headed out.

The bar was just up the street, and he would open alone as usual. Gus fired up the grill, turned on the salamander and deep fryer, swept and mopped the floor, and brought down the chairs and barstools. He wiped down the bar and reattached the soda nozzles to their handles.

As he worked, his usual first couple of the day came in for their afternoon vodka tonics. "Hey, Gus," they greeted him warmly. These two were really nice and enjoyed chatting with Gus about anything, engaging in small talk.

"What's going on Tom, what's up Jen?"

"Oh, you know, the usual. What do you say, Gus?"

"Not much," Gus replied, knowing that these guys weren't likely interested in his personal dramas. "Two vodka tonics and two Cokes," Gus said as he placed their drinks on a pair of cocktail napkins on the bar.

Tom looked and sounded almost exactly like Norm

Macdonald, which made it feel like you knew him. Jen was more average in comparison, but not to Tom. They were really fun to watch, as their sense of humor and mannerisms were nearly identical. Whether you knew it or not, it was obvious they had been together forever.

"What'd ya think of that cop shooting that guy?" asked Tom, while Jen followed up, "Yeah, that was pretty crazy, huh?"

"You know me, guys, never liked the cops," Gus grinned as he cleaned the rim of a wine glass from some lingering lipstick. "Yeah?" snickered Tom. "Yeah, I never liked the cops either, ya know? Her cousin is a cop though, he's okay." Jen smiled and said with a laugh, "Oh Tom, you're so full of shit. You never liked Kevin."

"yeah… cops," Tom followed up.

"You guys mind if I step out for a smoke real quick?" asked Gus.

"Of course not, go right ahead." Tom checked his drink.

Gus stood outside and looked around at all the things he's looked at every time he had a smoke. He watched the people come in and out of the Gym next door, and watched the traffic go by. He spotted some more regulars rolling into the parking lot and decided he better really get his game face on and went back around the bar.

"How come you aren't wearing your shirt?" asked Tom promptly with a grin.

"$20 Bucks?"

"Yeah, ha-ha," his boss had given him a pink shirt

that stated, "I'm not gay but $20 is $20," being that this had become, in fact, a gay bar. Gus topped off Tom and Jen's glasses with vodka. "$20 is $20," Tom chuckled again, as Jen stated, "Oh, stop it, that's enough." It seems like every time these guys come in, Tom makes a point to tell Gus that he doesn't have a problem with gay people. You could tell Jen was a little embarrassed, but I think we all appreciated that he was trying to be very accepting. He was raised Catholic, and the idea of acceptance and equality was beaten out of his knuckles by the sisters at a very young age. He was an old dog learning new tricks. It was almost sweet.

While all this conversation was happening, a few of the guys stumbled into the bar with their usual gravitas, "heyyyyyy." Mondays were funny at the bar. It was as though everyone was content and replenished from the weekend, while weeknights served as mini-weekends for everyone after work. The mood was generally high, and based on the number of patrons, one might think it was a Friday. The atmosphere oddly brought Gus out of his funk, and he appreciated the regularity of this place. It felt kind of like home as familiar faces started rolling in, and the first round at the bar was always the craziest. Usually, about 20 or 30 guys rushed in all at once, eager for their first cocktail. He topped off Jen and Tom's last round and started setting up drinks for everyone as they rolled in. He didn't have to ask what anyone wanted because they always ordered the same drinks. The few guys who switched it up every once in a while, were quickly asked which drink they were having to start the night. No matter how long you tended the bar, this hour was always a blur. The clientele's excitement, the contrast from quiet to loud and the sheer amount of drinks poured would always set you on autopilot. Regulars would talk to you, and you'd smile and nod not having heard a word they said. Usually, a couple of shots would be added for you during this hour. Those shots also had little effect on you. You were a robot, a bartending machine. Then you heard something that put everything into slow motion.

"How's Lily been?"

Gus looked up at Peter and took a deep breath. He looked at Peter and blankly said, "I don't know."

Peter looked at Gus and said very sincerely, "something wrong?"

The bar had grown a little quiet. Peter was kind of the leader of the group. He was the rowdiest and funniest of the bunch. People really liked him but mostly bitched about him behind his back.

"I dunno man, she kind of disappeared a couple of nights ago."

"What? Oh man, I'm sorry. What did you do?"

This was the line that put all the guys into razz mode. One after another they rattled off one liners regarding why Lily would have disappeared."

"Did she finally realize what she was dating?"

"Maybe she got a whiff of his cologne."

"I like your cologne, honey!"

"No, you don't"

"I do on him!"

"Maybe you just need somebody who appreciates you."

"You finally slept with her, huh?"

"Maybe you should have learned how to pour a drink."

And on and on and on.

Gus didn't hate it. He was used to it. He was numb to it. Sometimes it was really fucking annoying and sometimes it was really fucking funny. Mostly he was numb to it. "Awe, come on honey, she probably just needed a breather. We all know how she gets," said Peter. "She was always pretty darn independent."

Gus was into round two of the group's drinks. The good thing was that on Monday's the guys didn't order a lot of food. That relieved him from running back and forth to the kitchen. If anything, it might be a couple orders of fried foods that the group would share. As he was slinging this round Stacia and Chick walked into the bar. Peter ran over to Stacia and gave her a hug. "We heard about Lily, and we hope she's okay."

Meanwhile, Donny slung his arm around Chick, "Hello you fine thing, what's your name?"

"Ha-ha, you can call me Chick." They had apparently taken to the name.

"Chick, ooh, I like you. Let me buy you a drink."

"Yeah, cool man," they both winked and smiled.

Stacia and Chick perched up on a pair of stools at the bar and quickly began to examine Gus. Gus nodded hello as he poured them drinks.

Chapter 31 - Problemo Grande

As the door to El Rancho Grande swung open, it flooded the dimly lit bar with blinding sunlight. T-shirt cabrón and his brother strolled in and walked up to Miguel, ordering two shots of tequila.

"What's going on, what's wrong?" Miguel showed concern.

"Juan was stabbed."

"At the cell phone store, a girl just started stabbing him in his stomach," said Diego, our t-shirt cabrón.

Miguel poured them their shots and asked, "What the fuck are you saying, man?"

"Juan was hitting on this white girl, and she pulled out a knife and just started sticking him. We just dropped him at the ER. She took off and left him to die, man!"

Miguel, aware of most things, recalled his patrona bonita pulling out a knife and quickly wiping it off. "White girl, blonde hair, average height?"

"Yes, amigo, she had a backpack. Muy guapo."

"No, man, she was just in here! She's at the Desert Hills!"

"Luis, let's go, let's get her!"

They raced down Route 66 and pulled into the parking lot at Desert Hills. Bursting into the front desk area, the two men locked eyes with the woman at the desk and asked, toning down their urgency, "We are looking for a blonde woman who is staying here. Have you seen her?"

The woman behind the desk said with a stern face. "You know I can't tell you that."

"Lady, you better fucking tell us."

"Yeah? Or what?"

"Or we'll fucking cut you," Diego thought himself Tuco from Breaking Bad.

"Get the fuck out of here."

"where is the fucking girl!" He waved the knife around near her face.

"She lifted her hand from under the desk revealing a .38 revolver. "I said, get the fuck out of here," she calmly stated again.

"Let's get out of here, amigo, this gringa is crazy too."

They backed out of the lobby, stumbling over the door frame. She had the gun pointed right at Diego's head. She walked around the counter and followed them out into the parking lot. Lily emerged from her room for a smoke, and upon seeing the commotion, started yelling. Meanwhile, Diego began walking towards Lily with the knife. The woman from the front desk fired a shot that miraculously hit Diego in the calf. "What the fuck!" Luis shouted, running over to D, throwing him over his shoulders, and limping back to the car. "You're fucking crazy! You're fucking crazy!" With the gun still pointed in their direction, he pushed Diego into the passenger seat and scurried clumsily into the driver's seat. "Fuck you!"

he yelled and peeled out of the parking lot towards the hospital.

Pat looked at Lily with the .38 at her hip. "What the fuck did you do to those guys, honey?"

"I stabbed their friend," she said quietly.

"You can stay, but you might just want to get out of here."

"Yeah," Lily responded. "Thanks for your help," she said quietly, lifting her eyes towards Pat.

"Honey, I've been here 40 years. This ain't my first rodeo, ha ha," she said, turning to head back to her desk and wait for the cops.

Lily entered her room and sat down on the bed. Part of her wanted to just go home, but the stubborn part quickly threw a blanket over the emotion and set her back on the path of forward momentum. She threw her things in her bag, looked around the room, and headed out to her car. As she pulled out of the parking lot, she saw the police pulling in. Pat was waiting to give an explanation to the cops. Lily shared brief eye contact with them and took a left turn, heading back towards the Waffle House and the highway.

"What the fuck? Am I in a fucking movie?" she muttered to herself.

She merged onto I-44 Oklahoma City and continued on to 75 South. Eventually, she exited into a familiar place - a residential shopping area that included Target, Marshalls, Buffalo Wild Wings, and Whataburger. These places, despite their obnoxiousness, felt like home because of their consistency. She thought it might be a good idea to stop at the QuikTrip, top off her gas, clean up, and reset. She pictured herself at B-Dubs, eating some wings and blanking out for a while. She pulled off the road and into the gas station, where people were everywhere. Just people doing things like getting gas, grabbing a snack, pit-stopping for average things with average thoughts in average cars.

She perched up in a booth seat at B-Dubs and was promptly greeted by a friendly server. After ordering a coke and a plate of wings, she placed her bag on her lap and set her map and new cell phone on the table. Her gaze momentarily flicked to her old phone in the bag before she looked away. Opening up Google Maps on her new phone, she watched as it zoomed in on her location. Despite the lingering effects of the tequila shots, she knew she needed to clear her head before moving forward. Lily made the decision to take a break, enjoy her meal, and gather her thoughts. She needed to figure some shit out.

Chapter 32 - One Star Night

As Lily's head cleared, she decided that getting as far away from Tulsa as possible was the best course of action. Tulsa was a fucking train wreck, and all she wanted was to enjoy the town and catch her breath for a little while. She could never get used to guys messing up her life for a little attention. To her, it was no different than a cop shooting a black man for a taillight. It was always so volatile and violent.

Lily couldn't help but ponder the nature of those in positions of authority or those fucking alpha males who felt the need to provoke outcomes that ruin everyone's day, week, or even life. To her, it seemed too random and spontaneous, and she couldn't understand why they couldn't just let people be. It made more sense for dogs to fight for a top slot in their world, but killing to breed or rank up in a "force" was ridiculous. As she drove down 75 South, these thoughts swirled in her head.

She threw on the radio and fidgeted with the dial. She found a station: "Revive Your Testosterone," an advertisement came from the speakers. "Fuck your testosterone!" shouted Lily in the direction of the unit. "Z-104.5 The Edge," Coldplay's "Viva La Vida" came on. Lily hates Coldplay but left the station on. She was dancing a little in her seat while lip-syncing the words.

She didn't know any of the words. She realized she was speeding 95 miles per hour and promptly slowed the car down. She wasn't sure where the tequila would blow right now and also stabbed a guy. The last thing she wanted to see in her rearview mirror were the Tulsa cops.

It was going to be a long night. Lily didn't just want to leave Tulsa; she wanted to get out of Oklahoma entirely. She had 160 miles to go until the Texas border. She needed a coffee, and it just so happened there was an exit with a Starbucks right in front of her. It was a good time to make a pit stop. As she pulled off the highway, the cops blew past her. She wasn't even aware there was a cop there. This was a paranoia she didn't need to feel ever again in her life. She felt completely justified for her actions. The law would have to be considered a gray area there. She was threatened and acted. They chose to pursue her, and one was shot. She didn't want to be a prisoner in Tulsa, even if it was just to answer questions for three days. This escape was for her and nobody else. Anything that threatened that would be a threat to Lily's freedom.

"Tulsa doesn't have an amphitheater," said the guy on the radio.

"Fucking really?" Lily thought.

"Tulsa is seriously fucking strange," she thought of The Watchmen and the Tulsa riots. She imagines that bigot blood still runs through the veins of the citizens of Tulsa and had the same effect as inbreeding. She was certain that there were plenty of amazing people like Pat in Tulsa but had only her experience to go on. Why did Pat need that gun anyway? Was she a solution or a problem? Was she a female hero or a white bigot? Who the fuck knows.

"People are people, so why should it be," Lily sang the words out loud, "you and I should get along so awfully," as she tossed her cigarette butt onto the road.

The drive-through barista was a rare beauty, the kind of traditional looks that made her kindness feel both authentic and unique. Lily left a generous tip and got back onto the highway. The radio played a song that Lily couldn't place as being from the 80s or today but was somehow entertaining. Each song and commercial seemed to have its own unique charm, some were incredibly funny and could have been an SNL skit, while others provoked deep thoughts about interesting subjects. As "Last Kiss" by Pearl Jam played, Lily felt a surge of emotion and tears threatened to fall from her eyes. She wasn't sure if she was thinking about Gus, herself, or what she found of herself in Gus. She lit another cigarette and glanced at the speedometer, increasing her speed by a couple of miles per hour. She was making good time, and time was passing at an ideal pace in her mind. As she looked out the window, Lily was awestruck by all of the lights from the wind farm. Strings and strands of lights adorned the once-empty landscape, stretching far into the horizon. Despite this overwhelming sight, she was starting to feel free again. She'd be to Denison at a reasonable time for a good night's sleep. She was craving a Comfort Inn or similar and hoped this town would have one. The americana schtick was really cool, but it'd be a hot minute before she'd be into that again.

As Lily drove, she couldn't help but daydream about a comfortable and convenient hotel room with a nice shower. She didn't care about the retro fridge or any other amenities, as long as she had good movies and a quality bed. As "Cake" played on the radio, she found herself singing along to the actual words of the song. She thought about McDonald's instead of tequila and a facial mask before bed. The thoughts continued to run through her head. When she lost reception with the Edge, she ended up dialing in "MADROCK 102.5," which was playing a string of classic rock hits, and she indeed knew all the words to all of the songs.

"Welcome to Texas, Drive Friendly - The Texas Way." Passing over the Red River revealed a large 'lone' star planted into the entrance to a rest stop, welcoming you to Texas. She followed 75 and the Denison signs until, just after being informed that this was Eisenhower's birthplace, a sign for LaQuinta and an invitation to IHOP caught her eye. As she exited, she also saw a large sign that read Schlotzsky's. "I'll be damned," she thought to herself. Years ago, she'd eat Schlotzsky's back home when she wanted to treat herself. She would definitely have a sandwich before leaving this town. "Janie's Got a Gun" played on the radio as she shut off the car.

The motel room at LaQuinta was cool and smelled unmistakably 'hotel room fresh'. She turned on the TV to the History Channel and started to undress. After the events of the day that led to this ending, she felt so dirty, but she was glad she had pushed on. Her paranoia dissipated as the shower removed any trace of violence, sweat, and little bit of fear off of her body and, probably, into the Red River. She laughed as she thought that perhaps all the violence, anger, and fear that was washed off of everyone along the Red River, or any river that flowed into the Mississippi, were converted into evil spirits and were the reason all the chicken men and voodoo priests were fighting off evil in Louisiana.

Chapter 33 - Mamá Enojada

Back in Tulsa, Juan and Diego were lying in hospital beds in the same room. They were frustrated, while a couple of cops questioned them as both suspects and victims. Meanwhile, Miguel and Luis sat on a small bench near the window.

"You didn't know the woman with the knife?" asked one of the cops.

"Man, I never seen her before. I already said this." Juan was sore and anxious. "Why are you in here with us when I alrea—"

The boy's mother suddenly burst through the door. ¿Qué les pasa a mis chicos? ¿Por qué te metes con esas gringas? I tell you all the time not to mess with white girls,"

"Ma'am," Cop number two interjects. "If you could—"

"And you, you call yourself police and you stand here and treat my sons as though they are the criminals here. You should be ashamed of yourself! Can you not see that they are the victims? Are you totally ignorant to their wounds? A crazy gringa stabs my boy, another shoots my other boy and all you cops can do is accuse them because they are Mexicano. Why don't you go get the people who do this?"

"Ma'am, I am Mexican."

"You are policia. Go get this chica and leave my boys alone."

"Mamá, it is okay," Miguel chimes in. "They are just doing their job."

"And you, my son, you should have called me the minute you knew about this. Por el amor de María, how did I raise my children? Miguel, I insist you do your job and get back to the restaurant. You two, policia, go do your jobs. And you two boys, we are going to spend some time visiting Jesus. If your father could only see this, bendita su alma."

Miguel gave Juan and Diego each a gentle but still macho hug. "Be well, brothers. I will be around to check on you later. Come Luis."

"Hang in there brothers," Luis gave an equally macho hug to his brothers.

"You two," Said Mama. "Give me a few minutes alone with my boys."

"Mrs. Martinez —"

"I said for you both to give me a few minutes with my sons."

"Yes, ma'am."

As the officers left the room, Carmen Martinez gave her sons a look that put the fear, that only a mother could instill, into the hearts of both men.

Both men looked at each other and both pressed the button for the morphine drip.

Chapter 34 - Dress for the Slide

The bustling atmosphere of the bar kept Gus from spending much time with Chick and Stacia. The two stayed put at the other end of the bar, exchanging witty banter with the rest of the group. As Peter asked Stacia about Lily's cats, whom she shared a love for, Gus overheard and interjected, "I'm taking care of them," projecting his voice over the raucous voices of the busy bar.

"Once a pussy man, always a pussy man," Peter chuckled.

"It's okay, we'll break him eventually!" cried Andrew, one of Peter's friends.

Gus smiled and winked as he collected a few empty glasses scattered across the bar.

As 11pm approached, most of the group started to leave the bar. Stacia and Chick had already left around 9pm to go across the street, while Gus was eager to leave. He said his goodbyes to the last patrons as they filtered out and began his closing process. He had a smoke and counted his tips. The night had been a welcome distraction from thinking about Lily, but as it drew to a close, he found himself overwhelmed with stress, anxiety, and fear once more. He checked his phone, disappointed to find no new notifications. After locking up the bar, he headed back to Lily's place.

Roger and the cats were eagerly awaiting their food, water, and a walk. Gus fed everyone and took Roger to his usual spot on the lawn. He had a nagging urge to drive down to the West Side, near Jake's house, and have a look around, despite not expecting to find much at this late hour. He couldn't relax at the apartment and needed to distract himself. "Let's go, boy," he said, ushering Roger into the passenger seat.

They drove down Center Street and through the bar area. The streets still had some clusters of people in them as the bars were still closing here. He rolled through Jake's street and there was no sign of the bike. He thought he might drop into the coffee shop and look around. He pulled up to the front and admired the glow through the coffee shop's windows. He walked into a small sea of heads all participating in the usual dark conversation. Some heads were bent down over a computer screen while some were just staring off into space.

"Hey Gus, what are you having tonight?"

"The usual. A large Americano with cream."

"Any luck with Lily?"

"No man, it's been a long couple of days."

"She hasn't been in for any of my shifts."

"I know, she's definitely not around. I've been taking care of the cats and we've been searching everywhere we can think for her."

"I'm sorry man, this has got to be really hard. I'm sure she'll turn up."

Gus, no longer stalker-ish, took his drink and headed

back outside to the sound of the brass bell above the door. He was tired and felt lost. He fished a smoke from the pack in his pocket and lit it. Roger was staring at him from the front seat. "There's nothing here," he muttered toward Roger. He got back in the car, started it up and turned on the radio. "With Or Without You" came on as he pulled out and headed back toward Tip. Driving by he didn't spot any motorcycles and the bar was closed. He decided to make one more run by Jake's house. He turned the car around and followed usual routes, past Stacia's, back toward Jakes.

As he crossed the main drag, the radio started cutting out. He reached down to fidget with the dial, and as he looked back up, he caught sight of movement from the corner of his eye. Suddenly, the front end of a motorcycle collided with his front left fender. Gus slammed on the brakes while simultaneously bracing Roger to prevent him from falling forward. "Jesus Christ!" Gus went into a check everything mode as he tried to shake off the shock. He got out of the car and ran toward the bike where he found Jake, about 30 feet from where the bike lay, unnaturally draped over the curb. Gus bent down to one knee as Jake muttered, "What the fuck?"

Gus noted that he wasn't wearing a helmet or any real protection. His head was bleeding, and he had some pretty good road rash up his arms and his legs were twisted up. Gus was raging while still shook up from the initial shock. He grabbed Jake by the opening in his vest, pulled slightly up on it, and yelled, "What the fuck is wrong with you, motherfucker? What the fuck is fucking wrong with you?" Jake's head weeble-wobbled around as he tried to fidget his body away from Gus. "Where the fuck is Lily, you son of a bitch?" Gus continued to yell while Jake muttered, "Get the fuck off of me, get the fuck off of me." Gus let him go, stood up, and began to pace back and forth. A few of the neighbors of the accident site started appearing on their porches and in their yards. After looking at a few of them, Gus went over to Jake and kneeled down again. "Are you dead?" Gus whispered. "No man, get the fuck away from me," said Jake as he tried to lift himself off of the curb. His head was on a swivel, and the broken bone of one of his legs protruded through his jeans. Gus backed up a few feet and raised his hands, signaling to settle down. Gus could smell the booze on Jake's breath, which triggered Gus to look for anything that would make Jake responsible for this accident. "He's drunk, and he ran THAT STOP SIGN!" Gus said out loud. Gus looked down at Jake again and said, "One more time, man, where the fuck is Lily?" Jake looked at him and said, "I don't know what the fuck you are talking about. My bike, where's my bike, motherfucker? I need a smoke. Give me a goddamn cigarette." As Jake muttered this, a couple of people had now approached him where he lay. One asked, "What happened? Are you okay?" Police sirens could be heard in the distance and obviously heading toward this scene. "Motherfucker hit me with his car," mumbled Jake, not looking at the guy he was talking to. Some of the neighbors were taking pictures, and the dog was getting anxious in the car. Being that Jake was being tended to by neighbors allowed Gus to go back over to the car to check on Roger. "How are you doing, boy? You, okay?" Roger appeared fine. Gus sent Stacia a quick text that read, *"I just hit Jake on his bike. Total accident and not my fault. Cops on their way."*

An ambulance rolled up to the scene followed by two police cars.

Chapter 35 - Two Star Breakfast

The LaQuinta had a continental breakfast that included a waffle maker that made waffles in the shape of Texas. Lily made herself one while stacking a few sausage links and some fruit on her plate. She also grabbed a box of Frosted Flakes that she could munch on later. She headed back to her room with her food but also batted an eye at the swimming pool outside. It was actually a nice-looking pool and she imagined herself spending a couple of hours hanging out there.

In her room, she flipped on the TV and sat on the edge of the bed to enjoy her Texas-shaped waffle. The local news featured a variety of stories, including a weather forecast, articles about pets and their owners, an aggrieved property owner, a teacher of the month, the rejection of recreational marijuana, a woman who had shot her boyfriend multiple times, and ongoing war coverage. Lily couldn't help but notice that while the interviewees and people in local commercials had thick Texas accents, the reporters themselves didn't sound Texan at all. "Reporters always just sound like reporters," she laughed.

Lily didn't have a swimsuit and would need to run over to Walmart to get one. It wasn't far, and she wouldn't mind grabbing some snacks and some sodas for the room. She didn't feel hurried today and let herself know that this was okay. She threw on some jeans, her chucks, and a tank and headed down to the lobby. In the elevator was a couple in their late 60's who looked as though they might have been dressed to attend a party at the LBJ Ranch. The woman was wearing a one-piece jumpsuit with some western stitching on it and a few of those big turquoise rings. The man had a wool western patterned cardigan with a bolo tie and black leather boots. He held his cowboy hat in his hands.

"We're in town looking to retire to a nice little condo here," the woman said to Lily while her husband nodded. "What's a pretty little thing like you doing in Denison?"

"Just passing through."

"After passing through about 20 cities a year for 43 years I think I'll be okay to just put the rag on the bush," the husband continued.

"I don't think this one will ever settle down," the woman said. "We should have stayed in Dallas."

"Nope, I'm looking forward to the quiet life, Maxine."

The elevator door opened; the man signaled via his cowboy hat for Lily to lead them out of the elevator. She obliged. "Nice meetin' y'all," Lilly said in her best imitation Texas accent.

Lily entered Walmart and for a second forgot why she was there. "Swimsuit," she whispered to herself and headed toward the clothing. She grabbed the first suit that looked good and was her size and threw it in her basket. She headed over to the grocery area and grabbed some Pringles, some Mud Buddies and a couple of Monster

Energy drinks. She also grabbed a mask and some nail polish and a nail kit. She thought she might find time for a little pampering. Everyone here was very nice as she checked out.

She decided to take a little tour of town and stop at the Schlotzsky's before heading back to the hotel. Main Street looks a lot like most of the Main Streets in most of the small towns everywhere in the Midwest. This one still had an old theater called the Rialto which looked pretty and well kept. Most small towns have one of these. It's always interesting to see what a town decides to do with it. You could almost get a feel for the town's people based on the current status of its old theater. Most of the buildings here were clean and somewhat colorful. The end of Main featured a railroad track that probably served as a mainstay of the town for generations. She made a U-Turn and proceeded to the deli.

At Schlotzsky's she ordered herself a Schlotzsky's Original. This beautiful sandwich consisted of ham, salami, 3 cheeses, olives, lettuce, onion, tomato, mustard, signature sauce, and the most important sourdough bun. The combination of these ingredients on that bread was absolutely wonderful. She could hardly believe that any Schlotzsky's would ever have needed to close their doors anywhere in this country. She grabbed her sandwich and headed back to the hotel to the tune of "You've Got Another Thing Comin'" on the radio.

Lily settled in by the poolside with her Monster energy drink and a can of Pringles. She leaned back and let the sun warm her skin. Reaching into her backpack, she pulled out the book "Father Was A Rat King," a story of Soledad's survival amidst violence and bloodshed. The tale resonated with her, and reading it helped to prevent her mind from wandering to thoughts of home, friends, and Gus.

A small family emerged from the pool entrance - a man with a 'dad bod' sporting a swimsuit but no shirt and a gold watch, a woman with short hair, large sunglasses, and a beach bag full of essentials, along with two kids who appeared to be around 3 and 6 years old. Dad bod wasted no time and shouted, "Cannonball!" before running and jumping into the air, his belly jiggling. The kids' laughter, though a little annoying, comforted Lily. The mom set her things down on one of the umbrella tables near the corner of the pool while the kids tugged at her to hurry up. She sat down, removed the kids' swimmies from her bag and with a defeated deep breath began to blow them up. The dad swam up to the corner near the table and rested his arms on the edge of the pool. Lily watched all this without thinking about much. She was just staring through them. The kids ran up to the dad and he lifted them down into the water where they splashed and floated. Lily went back to Soledad who was about to off a guy. She wondered what the Tulsa news would say, if anything, about the violence that took place yesterday. She imagined Miguel, at the bar, wiping the lipstick off of the wine glasses and watching a recap, on the flat screen on the wall, of the events that occurred just down the street from the bar.

Lily put down her book and rose from the lounge chair. She could feel Mr. Dad Bod glancing in her direction as she walked toward the pool. The mom was already perched on a lounge chair in a complete coma. Lily descended into the water and began to bob around. The smell of the chlorine was pretty strong but was a smell that Lily found pleasant. That smell was generally equated to fun memories of splashing around as a child. It was also one of the more obvious triggers for traveling memories. She accidentally made eye contact with Dad Bod which was an instant invitation to small talk.

"How's it going?" he asked as he put his hand through his hair and wiped the water from his eyes.

"Good," Lily responded.

"Nice day," he said, while bobbing a little closer to her. "Where are you from?"

Lily responded, "Michigan." The man then replied, "Another bad year for the Lions, eh?" Lily half-smiled and did a dolphin dive underwater. She swam over to the edge of the pool in front of her lounge chair and drew herself up and out of the pool. She could feel Dad Bod's eyes following her as she lifted herself up. The mom was still in a coma.

Lily didn't want to talk to this guy and was annoyed that she had to retreat into her book to avoid his desire to invade her space. She took a sip of her Monster, put her sunglasses back on and re-entered the fiction that for now was also an escape. The mom emerged from her coma and asked Dad Bod what there is to do around here.

"I dunno," he chuckled, "there's really nothing here."

Lily was reminded of the Desert Hills and the

black guy with the cane. She was tired of her mind racing away from her. She turned onto her stomach, closed her eyes, and listened to her own breathing. She let the voices of the family fade into the distance.

What seemed like a couple of minutes later, she faded into the sound of a dozen people splashing, kids, and adults talking about football. She lifted her head and looked around at the visual representation of what she imagined when the noise entered her brain. Then, she turned over in her lounge chair and took another sip of her Monster.

"It's time to go," she uttered to herself as her senses woke up and the noise became louder. She got up to head back to her room, while all the dad bods and some of the moms covertly spied on her.

She entered her hotel room and flicked on the television. She proceeded through the channels until she ran into "No Country for Old Men" and Tommy Lee Jones staring back at her. This was a movie she could have on all the time, and it would only serve to comfort her. She had a sudden craving for Starbucks. "I believe that whatever you do in your life, it will get back to you. If you live long enough, it will," she muttered this sentence in her head and mumbled in her own words, "...or you'll just go on with your day."

Chapter 36 - The Coin Don't Have No Say

Gus had trouble adjusting his eyes to the flashing colors of blue, yellow, and red that surrounded the scene of the accident. He stood next to the passenger side window of his car, smoking a cigarette with one hand and calming Roger through the half-open window with his other. The paramedics were tending to Jake while the police were running plates and surveying the scene as though in a huddle preparing for the next play. An officer walked toward Gus and said in a calm manner, "Just give us a minute here, and we'll talk about what happened." Gus looked up while surveying his belt full of gadgets and badge. "Okay," he replied. The only part of Jake that Gus could see was his shoes as the group surrounding him examined and prepped for a lift onto a stretcher. "Just relax, sir, everything is going to be okay, sir," was repeated over and over from the group.

Another cop, Officer Rainey, was greeted as he approached the cop standing next to Gus. "Sir, could you please step up against the car with your hands firmly placed on the roof?" He motioned to Gus to turn around with his hands. "We just need to get a few standard things out of the way."

"Sure," said Gus as he turned around. He looked down at Roger as he placed his hands on the car.

"Are you injured in any way?"

"No"

"Are you in possession of anything that might stab, poke or otherwise injure me during the pat down procedure?"

"No," as the cop removed a small folding knife from Gus's pocket.

"Are you currently under the influence of drugs or alcohol?"

"No."

"Sir, would you mind turning around and facing us, please keep your hands visible at all times."

Gus turned to face the cops.

"Is your dog a threat in any way?"

"No."

"Okay, we are going to perform a standard breathalyzer test. Do I have your consent?"

"Sure."

Gus blew into the machine knowing full well that the couple of drinks he had during his shift would not constitute a high number.

"Have you been drinking tonight, sir?"

"Yeah, I'm a bartender, I shared a couple of shots with patrons throughout the night but nothing that should impair my driving. That was a long time ago, too."

"Okay, thank you. You can relax, "said Rainey.

Rainey was the spittin' image of a cop. He was in his early 30's, uniform was neat, and his face was clean. His hair was dirty blonde, cut short and neat.

"Why don't you tell me what happened here, Gus," Rainey said with calm authority.

"I was just casually driving down the road. I caught him out of the corner of my eye, and everything just sort of happened."

"Well, it does appear that he ran a stop sign and we do have alcohol on his breath. We'll know his blood alcohol level after we get the toxicology report back. The rider is mumbling some vulgarities about you, but we can't make most of it out. Give me a few minutes here." Rainey walked back over to his car and got on the phone. He also chatted with one of the cops that was talking to Jake. Gus looked at Roger who was sitting patiently while watching the action. Rainey walked back over to Gus.

"We don't believe you are at fault here, Sir. We are going to file a report and will contact you if we have any further questions. Do you believe you and your vehicle are in suitable shape to drive? If not, I can have an officer take you home."

"I'm good," said Gus, "What's going to happen with him?"

"He's going to the hospital at this time. We will continue questioning him once he's stable."

"Okay, thanks."

Gus didn't want to mention any of the stuff about Lily and the bar. In every way this happened to be a huge coincidence. Gus didn't want to put himself in a position of guilt even if, at some point, the cops put together the ironic connection. He wanted to get Stacia and Chick's take on it and work out what this meant.

"Thanks again officer. Sorry about the trouble." Gus waved.

"Roger, let's get the fuck out of here."

Gus drove away slowly as they lifted Jake into the ambulance and his bike onto a trailer.

Gus headed straight back to the coffee shop. He wanted to grab a new coffee (he spilled his in the accident) and collect his thoughts. He'd wait to check his phone until he was out of the car. He was now very intent on not becoming distracted as he drove. Something on the front of his car was rubbing on his tire. He'd address whatever that was at the coffee shop as well. Instead of parking in front of the coffee shop, he chose to park in the parking lot across the street so he could inspect the car. He got out and pulled Roger with him so he could use the little grassy area behind the parking lot to relieve himself. Gus put Roger back in the car, "good boy, Roger," and headed across the street. There were far fewer people here now, and Gus was relieved to feel a little breathing room.

"What happened?" asked the barista.

"I lost my coffee in a small fender bender," replied Gus.

"Same thing?"

"Yeah."

He took his coffee and headed straight outside where he quickly lit a cigarette and sat down at the little bistro table. After a couple puffs and a sip of his coffee he pulled out his phone. Stacia had called several times and nothing from Lily. The text message from Stacia read, *"WTF? Are you okay? Is he dead? Phone about to die... HMU!"*

Gus sat for a second and reflected on what had happened. "The sheer irony of it all. What are the odds of that motherfucker blowing a stop sign at the intersection where I was just fucking off? What the fuck are the odds of that? I suppose a little better seeing as I was only in his neighborhood because I am looking for him. Still, fucking chances!? Flip of the goddamn coin." Gus thought to himself, elbows on his knees, hunched over smoking. "The coffee tastes really good tonight. Thank god I wasn't drunk. That cop was pretty nice. Wonder what would have happened if I were black? Would Officer Rainey shoot me? I probably would have left the scene fearing for my life. Fuck them cops." The last sentence Gus said out loud. A guy at the table on the other side of Gus responded with a "Yeah, fuck them cops," while rocking back and forth. He had a small cup of coffee and the appearance of most of the homeless folks in the neighborhood. Gus tossed him a smoke and lit his second. He looked up at the sky and let out a pretty good sigh. "Where the fuck is Lily for Christ's sake!" Gus needed sleep again. He thought that tomorrow he might make up a report or something to the cops. Maybe it was time for that. Gus's sidewalk neighbor was still muttering out loud while the cigarette he gave him dangled from the tips of his fingers.

"Fuck them cops... der, fuck em..."

Chapter 37 - The Odds of That

Lily pulled into the Starbucks parking lot, grabbed her backpack, and headed inside. As she was digging through her bag looking for her money, a voice called out, "Oh my god, Lily?" She looked up to find the face of Lainey Holmes smiling from ear to ear with a very dessert-looking beverage in her hand. "Oh emm gee, what are the odds?" Lainey said with her coarse and somewhat nasally voice. "I can't believe I'm running into you right now!"

"Um, hey Lainey, um yeah, this is totally weird!"

"Oh my god I know! You hear people talk about running into people they know in the least likely places. Who would have ever thought I would run into you in BFE Texas! Where's Gus? He's going to die when he sees me."

Years ago, Gus had a brief fling with Lainey. He would always talk about how clingy and needy she was, as well as how demanding and bossy she could be. He would often refer to her as "daddy's spoiled little girl." After Gus started seeing Lily, they would, on occasion, run into Lainey at random events and bars. Despite their past, Lainey would always act incredibly happy to see them and looked for any opportunity to brag about some guy she was seeing, some trip she was going on, or some other trivial matter. She was pretty in a "looks way older than she is" kind of way, a way that doesn't "age well."

"Gus isn't here," said Lily, void of any explanation.

"Oh, well, is he in the car? He's going to die when he sees me!"

"No, he's not in the car."

"Where is he?"

"He's not here. What are you doing here anyway, Lainey?"

"I'm here for work. My boss wants to open a location here, I have no idea why. We are looking at some properties."

"Weird," Lily said, "okay then, It was neat and crazy to run into you!"

"Wait just one minute. How long are you in town for?"

"I'm not sure, Lainey."

"What can I get for you?" asked a barista.

"Triple Americano with an extra shot, please," Lily responded with a hurried voice.

"Okay, I will text you later. You're coming out with my boss and me. We'll have fun!" Lainey talked on with eyes as wide as they were able to lift those big, fake eyelashes.

"Maybe?"

"Okay! Look for my text! It'll be so much fun!"

"I'll be impatiently waiting."

"Give Gus a kiss for me!"

"Yah, okay."

"Cool!"

Lily took her Americano and sank into a chair next to the window. As Lainey pulled away, waving, and smiling like an overstimulated Pixar character, Lily immediately considered the outcome of this extremely weird and unfortunate situation. Lainey was probably texting Gus, alerting him to her whereabouts and pulling Lily back into the mundane battle between comfortable and barely comfortable. "I will need to kill her," Lily joked to herself, but she couldn't help but actually consider it for a second.

"Last night I watched *Sleepless in Seattle*." A couple of guys were enthusiastically talking around the table next to Lily's.

"Oh yeah?" said the other. "I've never heard of it. What's it about?"

"It's kind of a 90's thing about a couple, with that, um, guy. I'll think of it. He's in a lot of movies. Tom, Tom Hanks! That's it!"

"Oh, Tom Hanks, yeah, Tom Hanks. I think he's pretty overrated."

"Overrated how?"

"His, like, movies are, like, pretty good but he's, kinda, he's just always playing Tom Hanks. You know?"

"Overrated? I don't know. Name a movie he was in that you think is overrated."

"Um, like that one, um. I like that movie where he's a pilot. Then there was that breakout movie, what's it called?"

"Breakout movie?"

"Yeah, it was like where he played that kind of dumb guy. F... *Forrest Gump*!"

They both had iPhones in their hands and earbuds in their ears while discussing the fascinating yet apparently overrated movies of Tom Hanks. Despite the technology, it was clear that neither of them were afraid to hit the road and live that semi-charmed life of the 90s, cruising through the screaming trees.

Lily sank a little further into her chair, took a sip of her coffee, and let out a frustrated sigh. "God damn it," she thought to herself, "I could kill her." She stood up and walked with a defeated shuffle to an outdoor table, where she lit a cigarette. Placing her coffee on the table, she ran her hands through her hair heavily, as if trying to comb away her stress. "Fucking Lainey," she mumbled through the cigarette clenched between her teeth. She put her hair in a ponytail to trap the stress below the hair tie and away from her head.

Lainey was, in fact, driving back to town while sending a text to Gus that was definitely not in Lily's best interest. *"Hey, Gussy, I hope you are doing great and looking fine as always. I was just thinking of you! You'll never guess who I just ran into... Lily! I just ran into Lily Gus, Isn't that wild?"* Lainey assumed that Gus was in Denison and knew where Lily was. Lily wasn't exactly up front and clear about Gus or his whereabouts. Lainey put down her phone and cranked up the radio, dancing and singing along to "Shake it off, Shake it off" while the sun reflected brightly off her oversized, imitation Coach sunglasses.

Chapter 38 - Tom Mother Fucking Hanks

Stacia and Chick had left Gus's bar and wandered into a club down the street. "We'll have one more and head back to your place?" Asked Chick.

"Sounds good," replied Stacia as they bounced across the busy road. They walked into a lounge that had been promoting a spring break dance party. As they pushed the doors open, they stepped into a world they hadn't experienced in a long time. The dance floor was packed with people throwing shapes to a dance mix of 'Groove Is in the Heart,' as lights and lasers moved around the room intensely. Chick and Stacia pushed their way to the bar where Chick was greeted excitedly by their friend Matthew.

"Rae! Oh my god! I'm so glad you made it out!" Matthew loudly spoke over the music, the bass, and the ambience.

Matthew was of medium height and slender build. His face bore a remarkable resemblance to Tom Hanks, which made him immediately approachable and likable. He had a soft, intelligent voice that was also reminiscent of Tom Hanks.

"Matthew, meet my friend Stacia."

"Stacia?" Matthew said in a way that implies he

knew about their torrid affair, "I think you are absolutely stunning."

"HA! Thank you! Nice to meet you!" Stacia said over the room noise.

"What can I get you both?"

"What do you want?" Chick asked Stacia.

"I'll have a rum and coke," Stacia replied.

"Cool, so a rum and coke and a Two Hearted!"

Matthew had already prepared Jamison shots for the three of them, "First, a shot. To Rae and Stacia!" he toasted them both.

"Wooooo!" Stacia and Chick were both smiling and laughing, "Yeah!"

Chick hands Stacia her glass, grabs her beer in one hand, and Stacia's free hand in the other, and proceeds to drag her toward the dance floor. The air is hot with bodies, and humid with sweat, and the pair bob up and down while participating in a sexy staring contest. The place is filled with strawberry-scented smoke that is commonly used in strip clubs and maybe the mall. The DJ is clearly into 80's and 90's jams, and the dance floor is lit. Stacia sees some friends/acquaintances from work sitting at one of the tables near the dance floor. She grabs Chick's hand and sort of dances towards their table.

"Kristen! Natalie! What's up?!"

"Stacia, Hey!"

They both work for one of the boys from the boys club. They were nice to Stacia for the most part, to her face, but generally think of her as a fucking weirdo.

"How's it going with you guys? Mind if we join you?"

"No," said Natalie, "go ahead."

"It's been a while since we got to hang out," Stacia said as she and Chick slid into the booth. "Meet Chick, Chick, this is Kristen and Natalie. They work for a friend of my boss."

"It's nice to meet you both," Chick responded politely but with a tone of protective suspicion.

"How's things going with Dean?" Dean was Stacia's boss, Brad's friend. "Did you guys land the deal with Giordano?"

"No," Kristen replied, "He can fuck off."

"Common," responded Natalie, "we didn't get the deal… yet. Giordano is hesitant to invest any more money into the project. He needs to see a return soon."

"That's understandable," replied Stacia, "It's a ton of money!"

Chick realized they were out of their league but did enjoy listening to the conversation. "I'm going to get a round of drinks," They said, "What's everyone want?"

"I'll have a Rum and Coke," replied Kristen.

"Thanks Chick!" responded Natalie, "I'll have a Tito's Mule."

"Be right back," Chick headed to the bar to see their friend Mathew and assuredly shoot another round of Jamesons.

"Rae, I'm so excited for you. I like her."

"Thanks, Matty, give me another Two Hearted, two rum and cokes and a mule, make sure one of the rum and cokes and the mule are really, really strong. Like triples."

"You got it you sly little monster," replied Matty.

"Stacia and I have been too tangled up into this mystery of her missing friend or fucking that I'm nervous what a couple of boring dates would be like. I do not like her friends at all. I don't think they are really her 'friends'."

"Wait, what did you say? Missing friend?"

"Yeah, her best friend went missing at my bar a few nights ago. Stacia, Me, and Gus, he's the boyfriend of the missing girl, Lily, have been trying to find her ever since."

"Oh my god, did you say Lily? We were supposed to have coffee yesterday and she never showed. Her phone is off."

"You know Lily?" Chick was surprised.

"Yeah, she was pretty regular on dance nights a while back. I got to know her pretty well. We have a lot in common when it comes to movies and cats and things. We generally get together for coffee a couple of times a month. It's really strange that—"

With the force of a high-speed locomotive or an elephant, Chick's body was thrown against the bar rail so hard that they could feel their heart beating thump thump against their rib cage. The voices around them became distant as they turned to find the barrel of a spotlight directed with immense precision on a man, center stage, thrusting and jiving through the mouthpiece of a saxophone. The horn was squelching and squealing to a rhythm section that was both incredibly chaotic but impeccably in time. They looked through the smoky room, searching for Stacia among the barely recognizable faces. Directly behind them was a slow-motion and highly dramatic dance whose participants wore large theater masks depicting anger and fear. The pair twirled and twisted around in the smoke to the cry of the sax. Chick felt weak and warm, and their head buzzed, mixing with the intensity of the jazz and voices and this ritualistic dance. They could barely make out the voice of Matthew, who was yelling, "Rae, Rae!" from behind them. Suddenly, the distinct voice of Morgan Freeman, right next to their ear, startled them. "What do you think?" asked the voice, "Quite the shindig happening here." Chick continued to twirl inside their own head; their ability to interact or respond was highly stunted. Morgan Freeman's voice continued, "Almost everything you see here is nothing more than the astounding ability of your imagination to create a tolerable world that allows you to continue moving through each and every day without putting a gun in your mouth. Chick, we all need a little excitement; the outcome is simply the direction our subconscious is guiding us toward, the necessary direction of our evolution and survival. It's the guttural instinct of human nature that lands us not only on our feet but where we do, indeed, belong. Sometimes it guides us through the hurricane of a jive party."

"What the fuck, Morgan Freeman?"

Tom Hanks' voice resounded into Chick's other ear.

"It is a jive party, after all. Don't you think, Chick? I know I think so."

"This is ridiculous," Chick thought as they tried to focus on less jive and more on what the fuck was happening.

Stacia had run up into the vicinity of Chick, narrowly avoiding an elbow to the face. Two men were participating in a full-on brawl, which forced those around them into a ring. Matt had managed to pull Chick's barely conscious self out from under the bar while the fight continued. One of our contenders had a chair lifted above his head while the other yelled, "Common, motherfucker!" It was too intense to intervene as a single bouncer attempted to settle the scene. The music was still going, and the dance floor was mostly unaware of the contained drama. The bouncer, who was a pretty big guy, pushed the circle of viewers, which, in turn, provoked and herded the whole scene toward the front door. They spilled onto the brick street where the two put their fists up like they were about to start a turn-of-the-century boxing match. Prior to the fists, one of our champions had removed his button-down dress shirt, revealing a white undershirt 'wife-beater.' This shirt, paired with the nice slacks and brown leather wingtips, helped solidify the Jack Dempsey, turn-of-the-century look of this boxing match. The guy tossed his shirt, which landed directly into the hands of a midtown staple, Vacant Dave.

Vacant Dave is the epitome of rock 'n' roll cool. His macho style was that of cover art for a Hank Williams or Johnny Cash album. His collar was turned up on his punk button-adorned denim vest that fit nicely over his black leather motorcycle jacket. Vacant, turning to a guy sitting next to him and while smiling, extinguished his cigarette into the shirt. He winked, let the shirt fall to the ground, turned, and walked away. It was a perfect exit for a guy that existed as though life was a script. Meanwhile, our champions continued to yell and provoke each other with the usual, "let's go, motherfucker," and "I'll fuck you up." There wouldn't be a fight or an outcome. All of this would dissipate into nothing.

Still inside the bar, Stacia and Matthew were able to get Chick up and into a chair. Matthew grabbed a bottle of water from behind the bar and put it to Chick's lips. Chick lifted their hand to the bottle and was able to take a sip. The fading voice of Morgan Freeman continued, "Don't mind all of this nonsense, Chick. In reality, although it can, at times, impact our health, it is, nevertheless, nothing more than entertainment."

At this point, the room had spun and morphed from the juke joint jazz scene back to the dance club before going dark. Chick could hear a buzz in their ear as they opened their eyes, and Stacia and Matthew came into some focus. "What the fuck," Chick directed their voice somewhere between Stacia and Matthew. "It's okay, honey," Matthew tended to Chick, "there was a fight, and you took a pretty good hit. Take a sip of water." Chick sipped the water and lifted themself to their feet. "Are you okay?" Stacia held Chick's arm. "Do you want to head home?" Chick glanced at Natalie and Kristen, who hovered directly behind Stacia.

"Yeah, let's get out of here… now."

Chapter 39 - No Sleep But Need to Work

Stacia and Chick were heading back to Stacia's place when she decided to glance at her phone. She had several text messages from Gus but didn't want to read them just yet. She was driving and had consumed an amount that would definitely land her in jail. The air was only moderately warm as she drove toward home with the window down. She needed to get Chick into bed and look after them. This wasn't a terribly uncommon night out, but it was uncommon that the drama at a bar should so directly affect her. Gus would have to wait. Chick rested their head on the car's glass and stared out at the passing buildings, trying to recall the scene with the crazy saxophone player and Morgan Freeman's voice. Many of those scenes were now chopped up bits of memory that they didn't want to lose. Stacia lit a cigarette and offered a hit to Chick, who slowly obliged. They drove at the speed limit, which felt like crawling. When a cop rolled up behind them, Stacia's spine tingled with fear. She drove carefully, trying to be 'normal.' The real shitty thing about this was that Stacia had work in the morning. She'd gone to work while almost entirely unable to function before, but what scared her more was Brad getting a phone call from jail. The cops turned on their lights behind her. Stacia was terrified and began to pull off to the side of the road. As she did, the cop suddenly turned down the road where Jake lived. Stacia immediately felt relieved as she brought the car back up to the speed limit.

Once back at her apartment's parking spot, Stacia held Chick while walking them past Roger's empty saucer. Chick wasn't saying anything, and Stacia didn't know what to say. Both had enough stress, and life would not resume until they were safely planted into a warm and comfortable spot in Stacia's place. Stacia helped Chick undress while also undressing herself, started the shower, and led them both into the steamy bathroom. She felt dirty, and she knew Chick felt dirty too. Stacia wanted them to wake up feeling somewhat fresh tomorrow, so spending a little more time awake tonight would be worth it. They both got into the shower in the small bathroom. Stacia put some shampoo into the cup of her hand and slowly massaged it into Chick's hair. Chick, still half out of it, looked up at Stacia and murmured, "I love you so fucking much."

"Love you too, babe," Stacia said, after briefly contemplating the potential consequences of those words. As she massaged Chick's body and hair, she savored the sensation of caring for them, nurturing and protecting them. It was a new experience for Stacia, who had always been an independent tomboy, raised by her father to be strong and self-sufficient. She was used to being single and not needing anyone to take care of her. The idea of having to explain her actions, decisions, and movements to someone else was not appealing to her. She cherished her freedom to do, go, and say whatever she pleased.

In contrast, Gus and Lily's relationship was filled with constant bickering and domestic disputes that disrupted their lives for days or even weeks over trivial matters. Stacia had never been raised to fit into that mold. She was taught to always remain in control. But now, as she allowed herself to fall out of control and give in to her feelings for Chick, she was determined to embrace this new experience. "This," she told herself, "is me stepping out of my comfort zone. I'll be okay with it. I'll try."

They dried each other off and while pressed together, made their way into the bedroom. Stacia thought about Gus but left her phone in her pocket on the bathroom floor. She pressed herself against Chick's body and covered them with the blankets. The worlds disappeared as they drifted off to sleep.

The following morning, Stacia awoke to her alarm and the smell of fresh coffee and breakfast. She stumbled into the kitchen where she found Chick holding a plate full of eggs, bacon, and toast in one hand and a glass of orange juice in the other. They were fresh-faced and apparently full of energy. Stacia sat down at the kitchen island, and Chick joined her. Stacia took a bite of her food and said to Chick, both sincerely and with a little laughing smile, "This is the best breakfast I've ever had." They both chuckled, which forced some OJ out of Chick's nostrils. "Nobody ever made you breakfast, Stace?"

"My dad used to make me breakfast on the weekends. Those breakfasts may have actually topped this one."

"Well, I'm not your daddy just FYI. Sugar daddy maybe." This time Stacia almost lost her orange juice.

Regardless of the scenario, Stacia was still pretty tired and a little hungover.

"Aren't you sore?" Stacia asked Chick.

"I'm really fucking sore," They said. "I feel like I was hit by a truck and my head is pounding. I'm okay though. I'm glad I don't have to work tonight. I'm pretty sure I need a night to just sleep and recover. Stacia, do you mind if I hang out here while you go to work? I like to be around your things, and you have a better TV," they chuckled a little.

"Of course, you can hang here. You can do whatever you want as long as you don't watch my TV," she laughed, "and stay out of my nightstand." Stacia and Chick both laughed. The contents of that drawer were implied.

Chapter 40 - Hair of the Dog

Gussy woke up with a mouthful of Roger's hair as the dog hovered over him in his bed, eager for breakfast. The cats were both perched at the foot of the bed, staring at him. "Alright, let's go!" said Gus as he got out of bed. The three followed him as he reflected on the incredibly ironic and unfortunate accident from the night before. He looked at Roger as he opened his bag of food. "Do you think he's okay? I mean, he was pretty fucked up." Roger looked impatiently waiting for breakfast. Gus, opening the bag in the slowest possible way, said, "I mean, it's hard to say, right? Internal bleeding, brain bleeding, any kind of bleeding… A variety of shit could kill him, right?" He started to pour the food into Roger's bowl who was eating it practically still in the air. Gus continued to talk to the animals. "I mean, as soon as the cops ask him about the accident, he's going to tell them I've been looking for him. He'll probably make some shit up about all of it. He was going to get at the very least, a DUI and would probably do whatever that dumbass thinks up to get out of it." Gussy slept late today. It was 10am and he had to work tonight. He poured himself a cup of coffee and sat down at Lily's table for a smoke. The idea of worrying about smoking in the house was now completely lost to all of the crazy drama and seemingly random strings of misfortune that were picking away at his life. Today he had no target, he had no place to start. He didn't know what was next and was honestly too tired to think about it. Finally becoming fully awake, Gus grabbed his phone from his jeans pocket and sat on Lily's bed. He'd received a bunch of messages from Stacia.

"OMG are you FUCKING KIDDING ME?"

"You hit him with your CAR?"

"What the fuck are you talking about Gus. Is he dead?"

"Chick got knocked out at the bar last night. They are recovering at my house today."

"I'm working and won't be available for a while."

"I will call you as soon as I catch a break."

Gus text back, "Idk Cool," and sat back on the bed. He went to Lily's Instagram feed and began scrolling through pictures of her, pictures of him and random pictures of things that Lily found interesting. Ironically, he stopped on a picture she had posted of herself, Stacia, and Roger. Roger was still in his hole in the ground at his prior location. Gus looked at Roger who was lying on the floor next to the bed. "You better appreciate where you are now, dude," Gus said to Roger. Lily hadn't posted anything since she went missing.

For some reason, Gus figured that he would have to do nothing more than wait for a call from the cops. To him, it was only a matter of time. He was anxious to hear something about the accident anyway. He wanted to move on with his life. He craved boring days preparing for the bar, waiting anxiously to get home to a Netflix fest with Lily or just hanging out. He didn't like all this action. He liked a consistent, boring life. The last few days seemed like a lifetime. It was a very unfortunate string of events that should have been spread out over a month or a year, not a weekend. He had made himself a bagel and another pot of coffee while listening to some music. Roger needed to go outside again, so Gus grabbed his leash, and together they marched down to the yard. He had to work soon and had heard nothing from the cops. While Roger was doing his business, Gus was startled as his phone chirped. He looked at the screen and muttered, "Lainey? What the fuck does she want?" as he opened his phone.

"Hey, Gussy, I hope you are doing great and looking fine. I was just thinking of you! You'll never guess who I just ran into... Lily!

Gus's heart sank into his knees. It hit him so hard he almost collapsed. "Is this a fucking joke?" He quickly responded, "What?" after which he promptly called Lainey's number.

"Hey, this is Lainey. I'm currently doing something really cool and unable to take your call. I can see who you are, so no need to leave a message. I'll call you back!"

"This is Gus. Call me as soon as you can." He stood there with Roger's leash loosely in his grip and was then startled by another ding.

"Hey Gus, I'll call you back in a minute!"

"Fuck, shit, come on boy, let's go," Gus was anxious to get back into Lily's apartment and get this call from Lainey. As they entered the apartment, Gus's phone began to ring.

"Hello? Lainey?"

"Gus, you handsome, beautiful man, how are you?"

"Good, Lainey. What did you mean about Lily?"

"Oh Gussy, I ran into her a little while ago at Starbucks. Where were you? Are you here?"

"What do you mean, where is here?"

"Texas, honey. Are you not in Texas? I asked Lily, but she wasn't really interested in talking. We're supposed to hang out tonight."

"Texas? What the fuck do you mean, Texas? Where the fuck is she now?"

"Oh, Gussy, my love… did she not tell you she was here?"

"No, for fuck's sake! We've been looking for her! She disappeared a few nights ago."

"Oh, Gus, I'm so sorry. She's here in Denison. It's a little shit hole of a town. I'm here with my boss. It was really fucking weird running into Lily here. I mean, you hear about shit like this all the time."

"Denison, where the fuck is Denison?"

"It's about an hour or so north of Dallas, Gus. We flew into Dallas airport to get here."

"Jesus Christ, okay. Hey, if you end up seeing her, would you please call me?"

"Of course, Gus. Just tell me you'll be waiting for me when I get back. It's time for you to move on from her. You know that what we had was the real deal. Remember that."

"Okay, Lainey, just let me know."

"Bye, baby."

"Okay, bye."

Gus didn't know what to think. He was relieved to know she was okay, but what the fuck? Just left? To Denison? What the fuck?

Roger could feel Gus sinking and tried to get his attention. "Not now, boy," Gus said as he tried to call Stacia, who wasn't answering her phone. He flopped onto the kitchen chair, lit a cigarette, and felt what could be described as The Hulk's large hand squeezing tight around his heart. Every ounce of energy was drained from his body. He dialed Lily's number, but it went straight to voicemail. He could feel aches in every joint, every vein, and throughout his entire soul. His hands shook as he took another short drag off his cigarette. He picked up his phone, which right now felt like it weighed a thousand pounds, and quickly texted his boss.

"I can't come in tonight."

Chapter 41 - México o Busto

Lily decided that she would finish her day of pampering regardless of Lainey or any of that bullshit. She couldn't believe that this run-in had taken place. She couldn't believe her bad fucking luck. She drove back to LaQuinta while "Shiny Happy People" played on the radio. Somehow, the world seemed a whole lot smaller, and she could feel the compression in her head. It was as if her mother's curse, which she thought she'd rid of long ago, was still intact. Her father's voice was repeating loudly in her head, "I thought I told you where you'd end up, but you won't listen to your Dad."

Walking into the hotel felt different as well. She felt like everyone was watching her, and that this place was no longer foreign. She felt the familiar walls of home, all of her homes ever, surrounded her. All these people—the desk clerk, the folks waiting for the elevator, the guy eating a doughnut—were, to Lily, nothing less than everyone who'd ever kept her still. Their faces were all familiar and all held the same look of utter disappointment. She felt the sting of every needle that etched every tattoo on her body all at once. Lainey, that dumb cunt. Nothing would satisfy Lily's hatred for her right now.

After what felt like an hour-long elevator ride, Lily is back in her room, sitting on the bed, staring at herself in the reflection of the television screen, a barely visible silhouette of herself staring back at her. She had the box for her facial mask and some nail polish in her hands, but neither seemed like it would have any healing power now.

She realized that she needed to take care of herself, so she removed her clothes and headed into the bathroom, setting both on the edge of the sink. She turned on the shower and entered without waiting for the temperature to sit right. She pressed her head up to the shower head and let the strongly pressured hotel water run cold, then warm against her forehead.

As she stood there, she ran her hands down the sides of her stomach, around her hips, and along the inside of her thighs. She massaged the upper portions of her legs before reaching for the soap to enhance the feeling. She pressed firmly as she ran her palms down her thighs, as if to press the stress and emotions down her legs and toward the drain. The water dripped off of her chin onto the tub floor.

She hoisted her upper body backward and let the water run through her cleavage. She performed a similar ritual that she used on her legs, this time moving slowly around and under her breasts. She was involuntarily caring for herself while washing away the spirits that poked and prodded her skin. This was the exact opposite of what Stacia and Chick had experienced with each other some thousand miles away.

Lily leaned against the tile and let everything run from her mind. This little run-in had drained her of all her energy, more so than the cabrones and the lady at the Desert Hills. She felt defeated. She was Roger, on his chain, in his hole in the ground.

There was something provocative about her face, reflected in the mirror, covered in a charcoal mask. She imagined herself all Al Jolsen'ed up and running through a black neighborhood or giving a finger to a cop. She thought about the metaphors that wearing this mask could represent in her real life. It was stupid but, nevertheless, a metaphor for who she currently was. She was a white woman in a black mask, trying to escape that which enslaved her. She grabbed her nail polish kit and put herself, wrapped in a towel, onto the bed. She switched on the TV to the face of Captain Kirk in some cave-like structure with his away team. "Killers! Killers! I won't let you get me! I'll kill you first! I won't let you get me! Assassins! Murderers! Killers!" which Lily took as inspiration to continue pressing forward. She worked away at her toes, her hand moving with the arcs and dips along her cuticles. "Captain's log, no stardate. For us, time does not exist," said Kirk through the small speakers of the flat screen. "I need time to take a little break here too," spat Lily back at the TV as she continued to buff away the time from her toenails. She was sitting, fully exposed, towel underneath her, while applying a bright pink polish. It looked like cotton candy if cotton candy was smooth and shiny with a reflective finish. With each stroke of the brush and each very logical line from Spock, she felt less and less the blow from earlier in the day. Nothing happened yet; there was no private investigator taking her pictures, and no ninja SWAT team scaling the wall outside her room's window. She could, most illogically, pretend that running into Lainey never happened. She had finished applying polish to her toenails and relaxed into the rest of this episode of Star Trek. This was one of those episodes where our away team was on Earth, an episode where Spock wears a beanie, and Kirk is looking handsome in his pea coat. It was oddly comforting.

Somewhere between "no stardate" and 6 pm, Lily had dozed off, completely naked, on the hotel bed. She was a little startled when she arose and sarcastically said to herself, "Shit, I better call Lainey." She chuckled at this and stood up and began to dress. She was hungry, and it made her feel a little rushed. She quickly grabbed her bag and headed out of the room toward the elevator. Rather than drive, she chose to walk over to the IHOP across the street. "If there is one thing for sure," she said to herself, "there would be no Kate Moss at this IHOP. You only find a Kate Moss in a Waffle House." She laughed to herself as she opened the big, heavy door. Breakfast sounded good to Lily. In fact, waffles sounded really fucking good. The waitress brought her usual coffee and coke, and she put in her order. She pulled out her T-Mobile phone and began planning an exit out of Denison. She noticed that Dallas was not incredibly far away but knew she needed to be out of this country. This would impact her psychology the same way leaving the state of Oklahoma did. It would free her from the events with Lainey and put her back into a place where nobody she knew would know where she was. She imagined what it might be like driving her old Mustang through Mexico.

Chapter 42 - A Long Day

Gus weighed his options as he sat at the table, drinking coffee and smoking, but unaware of both actions. He was staring at his reflection in his silent phone screen. He needed some guidance or some kind of push. Right now, this is all so overwhelming, and Lily is so far away. He can't just go to Texas on this. He can't just leave. He needed an answer, some clarification, a fucking opinion. "Fucking Lainey," he thought to himself.

Gus's phone chirped in his hand with an unnerving volume. It was Gus's boss.

"What's going on?"

"I can't come in tonight. I found Lily in Texas. I need to figure some things out."

"Okay, Gus, I'll cover you. When you talk to her, tell her I'm pissed."

"Thanks"

Gus set his phone on the table and poured himself some more cold coffee. Sitting back down, he gave Roger another pet and continued to glance at his blank phone screen. "She left her fucking cats," he thought as he lit another cigarette. "I can't just sit here all day. I can't just sit here." Gus's mind raced back and forth as he waited for a sign. "I can't just sit here," he said out loud as he reached for his keys and pocketed his phone. "Stay here,

Roger," he said as he let himself out.

He rolled toward Stacia's neighborhood with the radio off and the window down. He couldn't seem to get enough fresh air into his lungs right now, and any direction he drove seemed wrong. He pulled up to the pump at an old gas station under the overpass to fill up, get some smokes, and stock up for whatever journey might be ahead of him.

As Gus entered the small gas station, he found the counter blocked. Jimmy had his magnifying glass out and was examining his lottery tickets while Fernando was creating and moderating another conversation about 'papayas,' 'cantaloupes,' and 'pineapples.' Gus's motions were swift as he parted the two and dropped his bills on the counter. "Twenty on two and two packs of Marlboro Reds."

"Guy be in a hurry," Jimmy said while chuckling and putting a small flask, he pulled out of a ratty, olive drab field jacket that read 'Rodgers', up to his lips.

"Probably problema con las mujeres. You do something wrong? You don't get no…" Fernando chuckled and made a thrusting motion with his hips.

"Yeh gotta be right with em," Jimmy said as he smiled behind his dark, taped up sunglasses.

The attendant laughed and made a cheers motion to Fernando as he punched in the gas and smokes.

"All set?" asked Gus.

"Cool man."

Gus ran out to the car, eyed up the damage to the front end, and started pumping gas while being reminded that he'd hit a guy.

He was already missing having Roger by his side. He could direct his outburst toward the dog which proved to be better therapy than any psychologist Gus had ever seen. "With Roger, I can hold himself accountable and work through decisions without a fucking third party," as he waits for a third party to help him find his next path toward Lily.

He put the nozzle back into the pump and jumped in the car heading toward the coffee shop. He waved solemnly at Larry and Paul as he rolled out onto the street. "Aaaaiiiooooooo," yelled Larry with his imaginary 2x4. His phone dinged and notified him of a text from Stacia.

"I'm so sorry Gus.

"I'm in meetings all day.

"Chick is back at my place if you want to check on them."

"Okay," Gus replied.

At Stacia's place, Gus exited the car and gave a quick and thoughtful glance at Rogers' hole. He made his way up and knocked at the door. "Who is it?" Chick yelled from inside the apartment.

"Gus."

"Okay, one sec." Chick was still in sweatpants and a sweatshirt as they answered the door. "Hey, Gus."

"How are you holding up?" Gus asked.

"I'm okay. I'm still pretty shaken up and sore. I've never been knocked out before."

"Yeah, it's unfortunate when things get out of control

like that. I can't say I haven't been on the receiving end of a bar fight… even the instigator. The shit that goes on. I'm glad you're okay."

"Right? It's a really strange feeling. You feel violated but a little cool," they both smiled at Chick's comment. "Not that I'd like to do that again." They continued, "What's up with the Lily thing?"

"I got a call from my ex who apparently ran into Lily in some place called Denison in Texas. Lainey, my ex, thought I was with her and was trying to plan a night out, so she called. She's been pissed about Lily since we got together. Lily's phone is still off, and I don't want to talk to Lainey. Sounds like Stacia is having a busy day."

"Yeah, she didn't get much sleep and has a bunch going on today at work since her boss was gone for a couple days. Are you serious with this Lily shit? Where the fuck is Denison, Texas? It's really strange that she'd end up down there and just not tell anybody. What the fuck?" Chick was putting on some coffee.

"I just don't understand, and I don't know what to do. Do I go to Texas? I mean, a plane ticket isn't cheap and I'm not even sure I'd know where to look if I was there. Lainey didn't imply there was anything wrong with Lily. What the fuck?"

Chick, standing by the coffee maker waiting for it to brew, followed up with, "So, what about that guy Jake?"

Oh, shit, yeah, I hit him with my car! It was totally an unexpected fucking accident. The dude was drunk and ran a stop sign right in front of me. I'm not even sure if he's alive. I keep forgetting about it after the Lainey call.

Every once and a while I wonder if the cops are going to call me or show up once Jake lets them know he's been seeing me around."

"Fuck! Do you think they can put anything on you? What if he's dead?"

"It was his fucking fault."

"Who knows what those cops will make of it."

"Fuck em."

"Okay, fuck em," Chick poured themself and Gus a fresh cup of coffee while feeling tired of the 'fuck em' mentality. They are exhausted and overwhelmed after last night's main event and wanted to actually take the real shit seriously for one fucking second. "Can we not fuck em, Gus? I mean, clearly your Lily wanted to take off and apparently doesn't give a fuck about her cats, Stacia, her apartment, you or anyone else. Clearly, she's being a piece of shit and maybe, just maybe, she's partly responsible for all the shit that lead up to you, maybe or maybe not killing a guy, and now standing in Stacia's kitchen talking all fuck em."

"What the fuck, Chick? I mean, what the fuck was I supposed to do? She was just gone. It's not like you haven't been all up in this shit since it started. I didn't know what the fuck to do and still don't. That Jake guy is a piece of shit no matter what and I'm still taking care of her fucking cats. What the fuck would you have done?"

"I don't fucking know, Gus. Fuck sake. The whole thing is crazy. Honestly, I probably would never be in your shoes. I've had a hard enough time letting somebody in enough to even start a connection. This thing with Stacia? This is an anomaly and fucking strange for me. I still have a guard up just because people have always let me down. All my life fucking Gus. I would never have let somebody like Lily close enough to pull this shit. I've been alone for a long fucking time because of it. I'm all 'independent' and shit, not because I fucking want to be! You are in love with an unstable chick, you cut the deck, man. It's always been your hand."

"It's always been Lily's hand. It will always be Lily's hand."

"Fuck the hand," Chick barked.

"Fuck the hand!" Gus repeated.

"FUCK THE HAND!"

They both kind of smiled at each other. They had become friends.

Chapter 43 - I Don't Get Ulcers, I Give 'Em

Lily decided to leave Denison and head to Dallas. She wasn't sure what would bring her to Mexico but knew she couldn't sort it out in Denison. She also didn't need to think about Lainey and all that bullshit. She realized that Gus probably knew where she was and was starting to feel really low. She knew that he'd do something crazy, maybe, and that it was only a matter of time before 'whatever it was' made its way toward her. She started to cry as she drove. The tears were big enough to make driving difficult. She realized she had slowed the car down to a crawl. She exited the highway and pulled into a gas station. The tears were an accumulation of everything that had happened in the last few days, the instinct she'd avoided for the last five years, and the emotion that comes with just being tired. All of this was triggered by that last thought of Gus.

As her tears began to subside, she punched, after a couple of tries, "Dallas" into her phone's map and surveyed different destinations. "God dammit," she frustratingly said as a tear dropped onto her phone's face and screwed up her map. After wiping the screen on her lap, she finally dropped a pin on a Hampton Inn that sat in the airport hotel area. She knew that flying was not out of the question no matter how much she pictured herself driving her Mustang across the Mexican border. She called the hotel and reserved a room for a night.

It was really warm, and the air was really dry as she continued to drive down I-75.

Chapter 44 - You a Long Way from Starbucks, Homey.

The nurse was in to change the gauze, check the drip, and make sure Jake was still breathing. Jake had just started to wake up as his nurse was taping up the wound at his side. "Ouch, fuck," he whispered with a dry and harsh voice. "What the fuck is going on?"

Nurse Johnson is a kind-eyed black man and built like a linebacker. With a soft voice, he says, "It's okay, you're okay. You were in an accident and were pretty seriously injured. You're going to be okay, but you need to rest."

"Shit, what happened? Can I see the doctor?"

"Yes sir, Doctor Bennet is your doctor. He's currently with other patients but will be in to check on you this afternoon. Just hold tight. Here's some ice water to keep you company. We have you on a morphine drip so if you start to feel too much pain, you can press this button," Nurse Johnson is showing Jake the controls and continues to go over the usual steps related to inpatient care. "Looking at this chart, from one to five, where do you feel your pain level is?"

"Fucking hurts," Jake whispered.

"Okay, homey, so we'll call it an eight. I'm going to step out for a little while, and you can get your bearings. Press this button (pointing at a button on a hospital remote) if you need anything, and we'll promptly send someone in. I don't think I need to tell you, you have a few broken ribs, a fractured tibia, and a punctured spleen. You've suffered severe burns up both of your arms, a part of your leg, and took a pretty serious blow to the head. You appear to also have days-old wounds that were also affected by the crash. You need to listen to me and get some rest." Nurse Johnson left the room.

Jake looked around the hospital room. It seems odd that he should be looking out at all this lush greenery out the window, considering the contrast to the sterile room. The morphine drip is good, but he is still very tired. He starts to lose focus while staring at the heart monitor, and the beep of the machine puts him back to sleep.

"Mr. Tomachewski?"

Jake began to open his eyes to an out of focus man in a white coat who is looking under the blanket at Jake's side.

"Mr. Tomachewski, I'm Doctor Bennet. How are we feeling Mr. Tomachewski?"

"Sore," Jake says quietly while still waking up.

"Mr. Tomachewski, I know it can be quite shocking waking up in a hospital after an accident. You've sustained some pretty serious injuries after you struck a car on your motorcycle. I should mention that your blood alcohol level was well beyond the legal limit. You'll be here under our care until we feel it is safe for you to leave. At which point, you will need to report to Officer Rainey as you will be charged. Do you understand what I am saying to you, Mr. Tomachewski?"

"Sure, yeah, sure."

"Okay, I can't stress enough how important it is that you rest and recover. You'll be with us for a few days Mr. Tomachewski. Nothing, at this time, is more important than recovery."

"Okay, what about the guy that hit me."

"I'm sorry Jake, can I call you Jake? I don't know anything about the accident beyond the injuries you've sustained. Anything else can be discussed with Officer Rainey. I have other patients to tend to, Jake. I'm guessing you are starting to feel a little hungry, so I'll send nurse Johnson in as soon as they are available. Okay?"

"Yeah, okay."

Chapter 45 - Cowboys, Baby.

After what felt like a very short drive, Lily passed the Dallas Waffle House and pulled into the parking lot of the Hampton Inn. She grabbed her things and headed into the lobby to check in. The lobby felt a lot like the lobby in Denison. The desk clerk was also familiar. "Lily Martin, I have a room reserved."

"Okay, Miss Martin, I'll just need you to sign here, your room number is 34 and you can get to the 3rd floor using the elevators just over there. Here is your key card."

"Thanks."

Lily approached the elevator and stood waiting with a couple wearing floral print shirts and flip flops. The woman had a visor on, and he was wearing a straw hat with "Green Bay Packers" on its band. Lily entered the elevator after the couple, who asked which floor she wanted.

"Three," Lily responded.

"Where are you from?" the guy asked Lily as he pressed the third-floor button.

"Michigan," she responded.

"Oh, you poor thing. We're from Wisconsin and always feel bad when we meet a poor soul from Michigan. There is no pain like that of a Lions fan," he said enthusiastically.

Lily wanted to stab him. "I get that," she said. "It would be nice to see a playoff game someday," she couldn't believe she just said that.

"I know what you mean. The Fords seem to enjoy running that team into the ground. Say, we are headed to Mexico. Should've been there now. We missed our flight out of Dallas and were forced to spend the night here."

"I can't believe we aren't drinking mojitos from Jose right now," Mrs. Packers chimed in.

"I know it. We travel to the same resort every year. The staff are great and feel like family. You ever been to Mexico?" he asked.

"Yeah, I was there once with my boyfriend."

"Well, if you ever get to stay at the Dreams, the staff is just the best. Just make sure and tip them well. If anybody ever earns a tip, it's the folks there."

"Don't forget about Oreo!" said Mrs. Packers.

"Ha-ha yes, Oreo is the resort cat. We make sure he's well-fed while we are there."

"We get him his own special treats!" Mrs. Packers appeared proud.

"Okay, if I ever get the chance, I'll make a go of it."

The door opened and Lily stepped out. "See ya," she said as the door closed, and she headed to her room.

It wasn't a bad idea. She could probably stay at a resort for a week and get her bearings. She knew the town of Puerto Morelos, as she and her ex had spent a week in an Airbnb there many years ago. She opened her room door and plopped her things onto the bed. Then, she grabbed her T-Mobile phone and started looking for resorts on vacation websites. She found the hotel they were talking about in the elevator, but when she saw the two-thousand-dollar price tag, she decided it was probably out of the question. No matter how much she'd love to spend a week literally worrying about nothing, she thought it might be a little extravagant for someone who just recently stabbed a guy. She put down her phone, clicked on the TV, and went to the bathroom.

She decided to make her way down to the Waffle House. "Another Waffle House," she thought as the elevator carried her, alone, down to the lobby. She walked through the parking lot of the hotel and adjoining gas station and into the Waffle House. "I'll probably think of that Kate Moss waitress at every Waffle House I ever fucking see," she thought as she was seated by a middle aged, overweight man. "I'll take a coffee and a coke, please."

Lily observed the couples in the restaurant and her thoughts turned inward. "It's not like I don't love Gus," she thought, "but our relationship was built on animal lust and passionate fucking. All these people, on the other hand, probably got together out of a need to fulfill traditional roles of mommy and daddy. You'll be my new daddy and I'll be your new mommy and we'll play these parts until we, in turn, become a real mommy and daddy. If one partner still needs to be parented and the other ends up in the role of caregiver, they might consider divorce." The psychology of it all bothered Lily, no less than the concrete and steel structures that shelter us from the sewers and rats.

She got out her phone and began plotting the next chapter of her adventure. Whatever it would be, it would start tomorrow.

Chapter 46 - Back in the Fold

Stacia's boss had finally wrapped up the workday. "You wanna grab happy hour?" he asked as he closed his notebook. "However much I'd love to, I really need to get home. I kind of went hard last night and need some sleep," she replied, twisting her answer into an afterparty that he could appreciate. "That's my girl!" he enthusiastically said as he stood up. "Get some sleep; we have a big day tomorrow."

Stacia knew something was wrong. Something had been wrong for a while, and it had been making her nervous. Brad hadn't been as straightforward with her about his current projects and was being a little too nice to her. The day's meetings were pushing all plans forward with another build. The buildings were going up fast, and it was becoming hard to manage the tenants in the finished buildings. Two buildings were currently still vacant, one was at final inspections, and the other was about 60% complete but stalled. After these two were finished, they'd have a total of eight buildings, all constructed within the span of 2 years from the first ground break. It was always a party, and it always felt good seeing the progress. Today it felt like something was wrong. The walk through the parking garage seemed to take a lifetime. She felt like she missed so much while she babysat her boss.

"Chick! How are you? I missed you today. Are you still at my place?"

"I am, Gus is here. He came by a couple of hours ago and we've been talking. He knows where Lily is!"

"Oh my god! Are you kidding? Okay, I'm on my way there. I'll see you in a few minutes."

"Sounds good, babe."

Stacia hit every red light on the way home. She was tired and wanted a 'normal' night. She was equally interested in all the crazy shit that took place while she was at work. She decided to stop at the coffee shop and grab some drinks for the three of them. She was doing this mostly for Chick. A surprise for Chick.

"Hey, how's your day?" Our enthusiastic barista greeted Stacia like a sales associate at Victoria's Secret.

"It's good, long day. I'll have three large mochas. Extra shots and extra whip."

"A little extra everything always puts a smile on my face, I could always use an extra whip." The young barista was smiling too big as he said that.

"Couldn't we all," replied Stacia. She looked around the room as she waited for him to make her drinks. She thought about the other night when Jesse was in here. "It'll be awkward seeing him after all this," she thought to herself. "Gonna have to move."

"Okay, here you go, three mochas with extra shots and extra whips," he emphasized the word whips.

"Thanks," Stacia handed him a ten and a twenty, "keep the change."

"Only until I spend it," same big smile.

Stacia kind of rolled her eyes as she turned to leave. As the bell above the door jingled, a guy, most of his teeth gone, opened the door the rest of the way. "After you, beautiful," he slurred. "Okay, thanks."

Chapter 47 - Rock the Casbah

It was a hot August day in the summer of 1998 when an Army recruiter spotted a young, relatively healthy Jesse hanging out just outside of the mall recruiting office, smoking a cigarette. Jesse's mother had battled cancer when he was only old enough to remember her essence. His dad had battled alcohol ever since his mom passed, which didn't help Jesse battle his way through school. He had barely graduated and spent most of his time trying to get a job that could get him out of his dad's house and out on his own. It was because of this that our recruiter friend only needed to spend about 30 minutes with Jesse to get him to enlist with the reserves.

In April 2005, Jesse walked off a C-17 and onto a tarmac at Kandahar. These guys were still casting the mud bricks, setting a solid foundation for a strong Taliban resistance. Army life in Afghanistan suited Jesse okay. This was his second deployment and, for the most part, he had looked forward to coming back. He didn't care so much for the heat and sand, but he cared a lot for the Afghan people he'd come to know along with a few of the friends he'd made in his unit. It was an unfortunate incident in the fall of 2005 that would find Jesse on the ground with a bullet in his hip. A group of them had left the compound and were heading through town for a rather basic training exercise. A car had slammed on its brakes in front of them and their driver, not paying attention, quickly cranked the wheel, sending the transport vehicle into a short wall and then onto its side. Jesse had been thrown from the vehicle but was then caught, by the foot, underneath it. The shock of the accident combined with the already tense situation with the locals, caused an Afghani soldier to fire a shot, which in turn saw an additional short swath of gunfire taking place. An unintentional and stray bullet found itself burrowing into Jesse's hip. Because of this injury, he was discharged and sent home. His home was his father's, who'd passed away in 2003 and literally nothing inside or outside of the house had changed in 50 years with exception to the TV set.

Civilian life wasn't easy for Jesse. He couldn't find work, survived on disability and other 'supplemental' income, while his hip caused him constant pain. The opioid epidemic made it hard for him to acquire the drugs he needed to deal with the pain. He'd become angry with the government, the medical system, and the general public. Drinking had served as both his psychologist and his pain medicine. He could feel himself becoming his father, but like so many other sons and their sons before them, he had no control over this outcome. So today, like most days, he'd wander into the kitchen and grab a bottle of Jim Beam before heading to the porch.

"Son of a bitch," Jesse said to himself as he sat on his bench seat.

He stood up and shoved his .357 into his jeans, squinting toward Stacia's car.

"Motherfuckers took my dog."

Chapter 48 - It's Always Rainey

As Stacia finally arrived home, Gus was parked in her spot, so she sort of angled her car next to him. As soon as she got out of her car, Jesse, who was on the porch, yelled at her.

"Where the fuck is my dog?"

"Dude, Jesse, I don't know where your fucking dog is."

"I bet you fucking do, bitch."

Gus heard the commotion and opened the apartment door to step outside. Jesse had gotten up and was walking down toward the cars. Gus stepped down and stood next to Stacia.

"I know you people had something to do with Tank missing. I fucking know it."

"Look pal," Gus spoke up, "we don't know where the fuck your dog is. Let it go."

"The fuck I will!" Jesse took a couple more steps toward Gus and Stacia.

Jesse pulled a gun out of his waistband and lifted it into the air. At the same time, three cop cars blazed up on the house through the alley, sliding to a stop on the gravel. Jesse put his hand up in the air while the cops flung open their doors and aimed their guns at him.

"Drop the gun, now!" one cop said while another cop told Stacia and Gus to step over by them. Chick opened the door and yelled a loud, "What the fuck, Jesse!" to which Jesse gave them a quick glance and looked back to the cops.

"Rainey?" Gus couldn't believe it.

"Gus, both of you need to step over here."

"Sir, put the gun down."

"Fuck you, cop!" Jesse yelled back.

Rainey tucked Stacia and Gus behind his car, raised his gun, and unexpectedly started walking toward Jesse.

"They took my fucking dog!" Jesse yelled.

"Okay, okay," Rainey said as he still approached Jesse.

"I'm going to lower my gun, Jesse. I just need you to do the same."

Suddenly, as though to say, 'fuck it,' Rainey straight up walked around Jesse, grabbed his wrists while the gun fell to the ground, and threw some handcuffs on him.

"Fuck you man, they took my god damn dog," Jesse started to cry while staring directly at Gus. A couple of cops grabbed Jesse and put him in the car.

"What's this business about a dog?" asked Rainey.

"No idea," Gus responded. "I can't believe you guys showed up when you did. What the fuck?"

"Jesse's been on our radar for a while. He's been dealing around town."

"So, you guys rolled up to arrest him for dealing?" Gus was surprised.

"Yeah, what are you two doing here?"

"I live here," Stacia said as Chick joined them.

Chick followed up with, "That fuck was giving us shit the other night about a dog. He got thrown out of the coffee shop."

"Okay, look, I need you all to please go back to your business. This guy shouldn't be bothering you for a bit. We'll keep you informed either way."

"Officer Rainey,' Gus said, "What about the guy on the motorcycle? What happened to him?"

"We got his blood work back. He was well over the legal limit and although his injuries were pretty serious, he'll be okay."

"Thank god," Gus replied, half-heartedly.

"Look, he'll be in the hospital for a few days. We'll give you a call when we sort out the situation," Rainey started turning toward the car.

"Rainey, there's something I need to talk to you about with that," Gus said as Stacia grabbed his wrist and mouthed, "don't."

"Gus, whatever it is will have to wait. I have to get Jesse here down to the station and processed. You have my number. Call me."

Rainey got into his car and Stacia, Chick and Gus were left standing there with three large mochas, extra shots, and extra whip.

Chapter 49 - Three Whips

Gus, Stacia, and Chick worked their way up into the apartment and into Stacia's living room. The three of them sat down as if their legs could no longer support their bodies. All three of them took a sip of their mocha at the same time and sat speechless for at least a minute before Chick finally broke the ice with a, "What in the actual fuck just happened?" The three of them broke out laughing so hard that Chick lost some of her whip through her nostrils.

"Did Jesse just get arrested? Did that really happen?" Gus asked with a smirk.

"Gus," Stacia responded, "What about his fucking dog?"

"What dog? I don't know nothing about no dog!" Gus said while still laughing.

"Gus, so you tried to kill Jake?" Stacia followed up in the same humorous vein.

"I sure did! You should have seen him lying there on the ground all twisted up. 'My bike, where's my bike?' he kept yelling. Dumb fuck."

"Did you ask him about Lily?"

"I tried to. He wasn't exactly in his right mind. I don't think he knew what I was talking about. I thought for sure he was going to die, and I'd lose my only link to her. Motherfucker didn't have anything to do with Lily beyond being a jackass at the bar."

Stacia, still a little lost, "So what about Lily? You hear from her?"

"Not quite, apparently, she ran into my ex in some town called Denison in Texas. My ex called me, thinking I was there with Lily, to hang out. She didn't have anything beyond that."

"Oh, my fucking god. So, she left? She left her fucking cats?"

"I don't know. All I know is she's in Texas and I don't wanna go to Texas."

"How can you not?"

"And what, just drive around? Who knows if she's even still there. I mean, how the fuck am I even going to get to Texas? I don't have enough money for any of that. I'm sure she knows that Lainey would call me immediately. It's gotta be obvious that I know where she is. What I don't understand is why and what's the reason for not letting us know what the fuck is going on?"

"Right?" Stacia asks, "And you know what? I'm her fucking friend. I was out with her at the bar the night she took off. You'd think that she'd at least shoot me a text like 'I'm leaving forever, peace out' or some shit. Didn't she think we'd all freak out? Holy fucking selfish."

Chick put in their two cents, "You guys, I know it sucks but who knows what she needs? Maybe it was either run or kill herself, run or be killed, run, or lose her fucking mind! Guys, what if the whole reason she took off was because Gus cooks shitty stir fry? I mean, Gus, were there no warning signs?"

"Fuck no, there were no warning signs! We were like a team, for Christ's sake. We were a pretty good team, I think. I mean, who the fuck just up and leaves everything behind? Who the fuck does that?! Five years I thought we were in a good place. Five years I've spent keeping us solid while working at the bar. Fuck no, there were no warning signs."

As Gus grew near the end of his string of rants, Stacia went into the other room and put on some 311 before resurfacing with a bottle of Tito's. "Guys, it's been a really, really long couple of days. Who wants a shot?!" Chick gave an enthusiastic "fuck yeah," while Gus simply got up and retrieved some glasses from the cupboard. Stacia poured three, three-finger shots, set the bottle on the table, and took a smoke out of Gus's pack of cigarettes.

"Salud," she said as the three tapped their glasses to the table and drank.

"Fucking Salud."

Chapter 50 - The Final Frontier

As Lily looked toward the horizon through the terminal's massive window, a string of glowing satellites appeared, cluttering up the vast expanse of space that was once reserved for imagination. While she found it cool, the sight also unnerved her. Also, unnerving is that in just five hours, the last five years of Lily's life will become chapters from a different book. She took a sip of her 'airport expensive' Starbucks, turned, and headed toward a seat.

Lily smiled as a little dark-haired girl with bangs and big brown eyes played peek-a-boo with her from behind the seat in front of her. She couldn't help but wonder what it would have been like to fly at such a young age. She reached into her bag and pulled out her iPad, ready to distract herself from the memories.

Earlier, between a Waffle House and the airport, Lily had made the difficult decision to sell her Mustang. While the car had provided her with freedom in the States, it would be nothing more than a burden in her new life in Mexico. Selling it would cover the cost of her flight and a good chunk of living expenses. It was also another history she needed to move on from.

Despite taking a hit on the sale, it was still a good chunk of change. As Lily settled into her seat, she couldn't help but feel a mix of excitement and nervousness about the next chapter of her life.

With the satellites still on her mind, Lily was reminded of the car that Elon Musk had sent hurtling through space. She visualized her own Mustang cruising past the moon and couldn't help but smile at the thought. After parting ways with her beloved car, she turned to her iPad as a source of comfort, allowing her to watch movies, read, and plan her new life on a bigger screen. Cozied up in her seat, she tuned in to an episode of Star Trek and tuned out the noise of the bustling airport. Her flight was set to depart at 6:30 am, just a few hours from now.

Chapter 51 - Catfish

Larry and Paul stood under the overpass, observing a backhoe and dump trucks maneuvering in the dirt. The temperature is a humid 83 degrees, and the recent rainfall has washed away the last crusty remnants of winter road salt. The surroundings have transformed from a dull brown to a vibrant green, yet Larry and Paul remain unchanged, unmoved by the passage of time and weather.

"IT'S A HOT ONE!" Larry said with the same massive grin.

"It sure is," Paul replied in his usual mousy manner.

"WE SHOULD GO FISHIN!"

"Yeah, it's a nice day for fishing."

"LET'S GO GET OUR POLES! I WANT SOME CATFISH!" Larry stuck his tongue out of the corner of his mouth and gave a Hacksaw style thumbs up.

"Okay. I hope we catch some fish though. I don't like leaving the river empty handed.

"NO SIR, WE ARE FISHIN' CHAMPIONS!"

Chapter 52 - These Americans

Lily wrote, "These Americans are truly lucky to be able to live the American dream. They can live each day completely content with doing daily chores, immersing themselves in various forms of entertainment, and existing to others as a profile picture and random string of comments. They just get by so they can continue to... just get by. Some stand outside clinics with signs that read 'God values every life' and truly believe that every life taken results in an innocent child burning in hell. Next to them, there are people with signs that read 'my body, my choice' who firmly believe that there is no hell. To each of them, they are right, and each of them are afraid. Each of them has a reason for war, and both of them have a lot of free time to stand outside holding a sign."

"Where does the flow of American money come from? All those joggers, dog walkers, project starters, and project closers just sitting around, watching endless marathons of TV shows. Thank God for the saving grace of television marathons. Thank God for 24-hour news, a channel for every bully motherfucker. Our forefathers forged the way for eight-hour workdays and endless entertainment. We have elections and food delivery options that allow us ample time to think about what to watch and ample time to watch it. We have cars, electric cars, gas cars, scooters, bikes, buses, and trains. We have jobs that pay us just enough to maybe have a hobby but not enough to turn it into an income. We have all-inclusive vacations with cheap booze and all-you-can-eat Gordon's food deserts. We have 'experiences' we can buy just a block from our house. We have it made. We have set it up so we can all be pirates, zombies, soldiers, and dragon slayers from our incredibly versatile, cozy couch. We can be theologians, philosophers, bigots, and assholes without ever leaving our desk. We earn the right to be right because we experience so much from our little screens. These Americans are lucky," Lily continues to write, "but not me. I need proof of my own fucking existence, or I don't exist at all."

Lily entered this into the journal she'd always had in her bag, a journal that chronicles all of the times she's set out for proof.

Goodbye letters to everyone she'd left.

Epilogue - Those Americans

Several months had passed. The gas station under the overpass was gone but the coffee shop down the street was still full of the same people and the same shitty art. The entire world was still a little warmer and the weather a little bit weirder. Some guys were still getting shot by cops while other guys still shot into crowds. The bars still had the same patrons, having the same conversations over the same exact drinks.

Chick and Stacia moved into a new place just a block away from Stacia's old place. Stacia found a new job after Brad's enterprise of overpriced apartment buildings failed to adequately satisfy the investors' needs. She is now wearing all the hats for another entrepreneur, a business partner who goes by the name Chick. Together, they are going to open the coolest little taqueria in town. Two of the boys from the boy's club invested in their restaurant albeit inadvertently through a startup fund. Regardless, fuck the boy's club and all the bullshit that comes with it.

Gus was perched on Lily's couch, watching an episode of Homicide with Roger. While Detective John Munch spoke of all his ex-wives, Gus's phone started to ring. He looked at Roger, then leaned over to glance at the screen.

"Unknown Number - Quintana Roo, Mexico."

He pressed the answer button.

"Lily?"

Book 2 - Those Americans

Coming Soon

ABOUT THE AUTHOR

Aaron Schaut is an Escanaba, Michigan native, who currently resides in Grand Rapids. He is a web developer, graphic designer, and struggling musician called Dynaflo - dynaflomusic.com.

While home, he is surrounded by the many animals of Michele's Rescue - michelesrescue.com.